Almost Perfect,
but Mostly Not

Vasudha Sahgal is an author, freelance journalist and screenwriter. Her storytelling journey began early—at the age of eight, she wrote her first story about a bunch of friendly witches.

She started her career as a trainee copywriter at Ogilvy & Mather, New Delhi—an experience she likens to being Charlie in Roald Dahl's *Charlie and the Chocolate Factory*: utterly fascinating.

Over the years, Vasudha has contributed to publications such as *The Tribune*, *Daily Post*, *The Times of India*, *HuffPost* and *The Quint*. Her short story was included in the anthology *Love in the Times of WhatsApp and Other Stories*. She has also authored two illustrated children's books. Additionally, she has sold the intellectual property rights to her first feature screenplay to a production house.

Beyond writing, Vasudha manages operations at her family's precision engineering company, Micron Instruments Pvt. Ltd. She is passionate about travel, food, words and our existence in the world. *Almost Perfect, but Mostly Not* marks her debut solo venture into short fiction.

Find more about Vasudha and read her poetry on Instagram:
@vasudhasahgal
@vasudha_poetry

Almost Perfect, but Mostly Not
A Collection of Short Stories

Vasudha Sahgal

RUPA

Published by
Rupa Publications India Pvt. Ltd 2025
7/16, Ansari Road, Daryaganj
New Delhi 110002

Sales centres:
Bengaluru Chennai
Hyderabad Jaipur Kathmandu
Kolkata Mumbai Prayagraj

Copyright © Vasudha Sahgal 2025

All rights reserved.
This is a work of fiction. Names, characters, places and incidents are either the product of the author's imagination or are used fictitiously and any resemblance to any actual person, living or dead, events or locales is entirely coincidental.

No part of this publication may be reproduced, transmitted, or stored in a retrieval system, in any form or by any means, electronic, mechanical, photocopying, recording or otherwise, without the prior permission of the publisher.

P-ISBN: 978-93-6156-785-8
E-ISBN: 978-93-6156-997-5

Second impression 2025

10 9 8 7 6 5 4 3 2

The moral right of the authors has been asserted.

Printed in India

This book is sold subject to the condition that it shall not, by way of trade or otherwise, be lent, resold, hired out, or otherwise circulated, without the publisher's prior consent, in any form of binding or cover other than that in which it is published.

Disclaimer: The terms 'aunties' and 'uncles' are used affectionately to address acquaintances, friends of parents and other individuals who are older. In India, these terms are commonly used as a mark of respect rather than addressing such individuals by their actual names.

For my parents,
who taught me to walk, talk and dream—and gave me
wings to fly.

For my teachers at my alma mater,
The Lawrence School, Sanawar,
who kept my dreams alive.

Contents

The Painting	1
Delhi Drama, Turkish Trauma	12
Forbidden	36
Elite Club	43
The Banker Cabby	59
When Life Gives You Lemons, Write a Novel	75
Serendipity, Lost and Found	100
The Khanna Conundrum	104
The Life of Three	118
Ten Senses and Sixth Sense	139
Six Feet of Separation	152
Tony de Souza's Date with Death	162
Natasha's Nod to Her Normal	173
Rinse, Reveal, Repeat	186
In Gratitude	197

The Painting

He still couldn't believe it; out of all his works—there had been around 20 on display—the collector had chosen that one. Sahil had meant to move it from the studio to his room upstairs before the eminent collector and billionaire, Mr Daulatram, arrived. But it had been nearly a year since anything had sold. In his mixture of desperation and excitement, he had forgotten to remove the painting. Now it was too late. The billionaire had kept his word. He had promised to pay Sahil a visit three years ago, back when Sahil was in his third year at Mumbai Art College.

The college had organized a competition and had had Mr Daulatram as their chief guest and part of the jury. Sahil had missed first place by only two points; his oil-on-canvas sunset had come a close second to Shikhar's abstract illusion. But to Mr Daulatram, Sahil had been a winner. 'You will go far, son. Carry on, and some day, I promise to pay you a visit,' Mr Daulatram had whispered in Sahil's ear before exiting the college auditorium. That evening, Sahil read up on the elusive billionaire, who had made his fortune by creating affordable white sneakers for the general public. Mr Daulatram's father had been a cobbler, and now his company was listed on the New York Stock Exchange.

'My father renamed himself Daulatram because he truly believed in the power of one's name,' he had said in his opening remarks at the competition. He had gone on to share his humble beginnings, telling the eager students how he was always 'hungry'. Sahil could relate—he, too, had always been 'hungry' to make a mark with his art. Much to his father's dismay, he had chosen art college over engineering.

Those three years at college had been filled with strife between him and his father. Now, three years after graduation, the struggle had proven even harder than his parents had feared. Sahil had become pretty much a recluse, taking on odd jobs to support his dream of becoming an artist. His parents were hard-working, middle-class people. His father had retired as the head engineer in a company that manufactured pipes, and his mother primarily a homemaker, occasionally provided private tuitions whenever the family was in need of some extra money. Sahil's sister, Sangeeta, had married a respectable NRI doctor, much to their parents' relief. She was now well settled in San Francisco, proud wife of a cardiologist and proud mother of two daughters.

Sahil knew he had let his parents down. 'What the hell is an artist?' his father had once asked impulsively, the tone jolting Sahil. 'In our time, there were only doctors and engineers, and those who got low marks became lawyers! Now even that's very respectable.'

Sahil had just turned 17 when he broke the news to his father that he had applied to art schools alongside engineering. 'We are middle-class people. We work hard to put food on the table. *Yeh art ka shauk paal lo, par isse koi izzatdar naukri nahin milegi* (This art hobby of yours won't lead to a respectable job),' his father had said.

The worst moment was when his mother, who had always doted on him and taken his side, spoke up at the dinner table. Without warning, she said, 'Why are you giving your father so much stress? Let him retire in peace. And besides, no girl will want to marry you.'

Sahil hadn't made it to a single engineering college, much to his relief. Now, he had no choice but to pursue art. If he'd had a choice, he knew what his father would have said in that stern yet soft voice of his. 'We middle-class people don't have the luxury of choosing such *shauks*—these interests—over the stability a degree like engineering can provide.'

It wasn't as though Sahil disliked science; he even suspected he could have managed engineering if he'd tried. But his mind was forever occupied by art. He saw art in the temple walls where he went to pray, in the sparrows lined up along the sidewalks, and even in the equations of physics—$E=MC^2$—while cramming for the engineering exams. He saw art in the way trees swayed to the rhythm of the wind, and on his canvas, he tried to capture their carefree movements.

The painting that Mr Daulatram had bought was inspired by her, from two years ago. Sahil had met her at the Chinese restaurant in Juhu, where he worked as a waiter. It was a July afternoon, and rain was pouring down with an intensity that seemed to release days' worth of pent-up emotions. Such were Mumbai monsoons; the entire city would be flooded for days to come.

She came in alone, ordering egg chicken fried rice, which she ate hastily but timidly. Even now he remembered what she wore—a flowing pink dress that reached her ankles, hugging her thin waist slightly. Her brown hair cascaded down her back, reaching her hips. She had plump, pink lips, and her brown eyes were framed by the most expressive brows he had ever seen.

'Will that be all, madam?' he had asked, trying not to stare too deeply into those eyes. She nodded politely, her smile close-lipped. He'd thought then that if he ever painted her, he would definitely ask her to smile with her teeth; he was somehow sure that would bring her beauty fully to life.

The second time he saw her was the next day, when she visited the restaurant again. A thunderstorm raged outside, and she arrived slightly later than the day before, around 4 p.m. An hour later, as his shift was ending, Sahil found her at the entrance, desperately trying to hail a cab. He watched her for a couple of minutes, and then, without quite knowing why, blurted, 'May I offer you a lift?'

The question startled him as much as it did her. She nodded, again politely smiling, her plump lips pursed together, as if she were afraid to say anything aloud. As she climbed on to his scooter, Sahil asked her, 'What is your name?'

'Sanjana,' she replied softly. She held on to him tightly as the scooter jolted over the first pothole and then, just as impulsively as she had reached out, she released her hold. Sahil still remembered that he had never felt anything quite like her touch before. It was bizarre. He had been with many girls during his college days, often amazed at his own promiscuity, but after his meeting with Sanjana, he knew things would never be the same again.

Sanjana had only been in Mumbai for three months. She had moved there from Pune, to become a model. So far, she had landed nothing. She lived in a one-bedroom rented flat not far from the restaurant, and dropped by to grab a meal every day between auditions. Dropping her home became routine. They would talk a bit on these rides, her arms encircling Sahil's waist more comfortably with each passing day. How he wished to talk to her more, to know her story, to paint her.

One day, he finally mustered the courage. As she was getting off the scooter, he blurted, 'Can I paint you? I mean...I've been looking for a subject for a full portrait for days now, but I can't afford one, and...'

Sanjana broke into a broad smile, her shiny white teeth in full view for the first time. 'I would be happy to help you out, Sahil,' she said excitedly. 'Who knows, maybe this painting will make you famous. And If I am still not a star, we can split the profits!' She winked playfully. 'Besides, I can't really say I have better things to do! I am still waiting for that call for a ramp walk assignment or a detergent ad.'

They chose Sunday, Sahil's day off from the restaurant. She came to the studio in a blue chiffon sari, her hair cascading loosely over one shoulder. She had worn a tiny silver bindi on her forehead.

Now I can stare at her without coming off as a creep. She knows it's just part of the job, Sahil thought as he positioned himself in front of the canvas. For the next few Sundays, he stared long and hard at her face; he didn't know then that that face would both haunt and bless him in time to come.

After the portrait was complete, in the days that

followed, Sanjana and Sahil became lovers. He often thought about that first Sunday when he had started her portrait; he had sensed back then that something would brew between them. Now, when he reminisced their time together, he never really saw her as a whole; instead, each feature had become a character of its own. He remembered the first time they kissed and how her plump lips melted into his. He had noticed her eyelashes up close then—the longest he had ever seen. When he showered hurried kisses on her stunning collarbones, he thought her neck seemed endlessly graceful. The first time they got into an argument, he remembered teasing her about her nostrils flaring up, an expressive quirk of her otherwise unassuming nose.

Creatively, meeting Sanjana marked his most fruitful period. He churned out a painting every ten days despite his day job, even landing a spot in a show for upcoming artists. Sanjana too landed a couple of auditions for advertisements. She could now afford to take time out for two meals a day. The six months he spent with Sanjana were the best time of his life.

A phone call interrupted his thoughts. It was Mr Daulatram. Caught up in his memories, Sahil almost didn't hear the phone ring.

'Ah Sahil! I was calling to tell you that I will have the painting picked up the day after tomorrow at noon. Hope that works! Also, I hope the amount I send will match the price you had in mind. I wish you had quoted something.' He then heard the phone click, as the speaker had hung up. Sahil didn't mind; he assumed billionaires were always busy and, hence, to the point.

Sahil had quoted nothing when Mr Daulatram had pointed to the painting. The piece depicted a beautiful young woman immersed in a poetry book, lazing on a divan, her long legs draped in blue fabric. Only Sanjana could have made that posture look so dignified in a sari. There was a natural ease in her face, an innate grace and hope.

It had been Sanjana's idea. 'Well, if this is going to take some time, I may as well read,' she had chuckled, her brown eyes lighting up. She had even come prepared, bringing along a copy of Kahlil Gibran's poetry. Then came the question of what to do with her hands. That was always the trickiest part of portraits. The way she held the book, her long fingers curling around its fading cover became Sahil's favourite detail.

During that week, as he painted her, they spoke a lot—about their fears, apprehensions and expectations from life. They shared similar dreams. Sanjana wanted to be a top model in Paris; Sahil wouldn't have minded a solo exhibition in that same dreamy city himself. They were both struggling artists with stars in their eyes. Their six months together were full of passionate lovemaking and equally passionate art-making for Sahil. *Is this what is heaven?* Sahil had thought.

Sahil made his way to the painting. He hadn't been able to look at it since Mr Daulatram chose it. The thought of parting with it had brought a pain—the sharp one that shoots up without warning when a painkiller's numbing effect wears out. He decided to allow himself one last glance before calling the packers. As he looked at it, what caught his attention were the protagonist's eyes. They took him back to the last time they had seen each other.

Sanjana, after only months of struggling as a new model in Mumbai, had landed the opportunity to model for a leading Indian designer in Paris. Her eyes had been full of hope, touched with a slight twinge of sadness. 'I wish you could come with me, Sahil! I know it's only for a month, but I will miss you immensely.'

That 'month' turned into a whole year. Sanjana was a bigger hit in Paris than she could have ever fathomed. International designers lined up, and soon, she was the face of an esteemed international beauty brand. Sahil was happy for her. He had always known she would make it. But the separation was painful for him, plunging him into a creative block. He produced no art, drifting from one odd job to the next. It was a year of mourning; even his parents went from being angry at his decision to being sympathetic to their son's plight. They had heard of Sanjana but never met her. 'When the time is right,' he would tell them.

For the first few months, Sahil was able to tide over financially with one or two shows, thanks to the works from the 'creative high' phase he had experienced with Sanjana. But after those pieces sold, his creative well ran dry. The following year, he found inspiration from the spirit of Mumbai's people, from other strugglers whose stories triggered his imagination. But nothing was really selling. No gallery wanted his work. Sanjana and he spoke occasionally in the early months, and he always tried to sound upbeat; he didn't want pity from her. Mostly, he let her talk, but she was never a big talker. *Her eyes did most of the talking*, he thought during their long pauses on the phone. Eventually, he stopped taking her calls altogether.

It was at a wine-and-cheese event hosted by a fellow college student at a reputed art gallery in New Delhi that Sahil bumped into Mr Daulatram. The billionaire had tapped him on the shoulder exclaiming, 'Look who I find here! The talented Sahil! I had hoped we'd meet again sometime.' That is when Mr Daulatram had promised to visit Sahil's studio. True to his word, he came to the studio the following week, once he was back in Mumbai. Sahil had great respect for people like Mr Daulatram—those who supported young talent and honoured their promises.

Mr Daulatram was immediately drawn to Sanjana's portrait. 'This is going to go up in the den of my new house in London! And I am going to send you a ticket to come and see it when it's up, my friend,' he had chirped enthusiastically.

The cheque that Mr Daulatram had sent Sahil was more than anything he could have ever dreamt of—₹75 lakh. He had no name on the art scene. And yet this gentleman thought his work was worth so much. He couldn't help but admit that the amount made him feel very relieved. He had needed the money and it also gave him hope. People from illustrious backgrounds were sure to spot the painting in Mr Daulatram's home. It was a golden chance to resurrect a career he had almost given up on.

It was a fine morning, and the view from her apartment couldn't be better. The Eiffel Tower gleamed in the sunlight slipping through low-hanging clouds, which looked like candyfloss. Sanjana had everything she had dreamt of, yet some mornings left her feeling inexplicably hollow.

She opened the door to retrieve her mail, and underneath the usual French newspapers was a courier from India. She tore it open. Inside it was a cheque in her name for ₹37.5 lakh, issued by the White Sneaker Company, India, which baffled her. Along with it was a note:

> To the moon he didn't compare her,
> For the moon was stained;
> Neither to the red rose
> For she hadn't the thorns and rough edges.
> He compared her to the reflection
> Of the sunset in the sea,
> For just like the orange in water,
> She was the fire
> That ignited his pristine soul.

There was no signature, but she didn't need one. She knew who it was from. The writer had shared this poem with her once. He had told her that he wasn't a poet and was quite sure that this was the only poem he would ever write. For the first time since leaving India, Sanjana cried hysterically, her tears tinged with both joy and sorrow.

'Who is this talented young fellow?' enquired a leading journalist as he gazed at one of the paintings adorning Mr Daulatram's walls in his Mayfair mansion.

'I must have his work!' added a middle-aged socialite in a glittering cocktail dress.

'Indeed impressive,' agreed a famous lawyer, who had been recently knighted by the Queen.

Daulatram smiled to himself. He knew he had a knack for spotting true talent.

It was his housewarming party in London, the evening filled with fine wine and finer company. Next to the portrait of the woman in the blue chiffon sari, a small note was pinned to the wall. It was a poem, signed by Sahil, the artist himself.

Delhi Drama, Turkish Trauma

Maya Khanna was a born fashionista. After a 24-hour labour, during which her mother insisted on wearing Loro Piana shoes because she always felt a little colder than others, Maya made her entrance into the world. Her parents placed her in a Fendi pram and whisked her off to their grand mansion in Lutyens' Delhi, where she was fed with a silver spoon, pun intended. Maya's first words were 'Goo-chee' and 'Praaa-daa', followed by 'Dada' and 'Mama'.

In the nature versus nurture debate it was probably a concoction of both that was responsible for her keen eye for style and her taste for the high life. Summer holidays were usually spent in Milan, Paris, London, New York or Vienna, where her parents preferred dining at Michelin-starred restaurants, looking at modern art and shopping at Selfridges or Saks.

While Maya inherited her flair for fashion from her mother, at heart she was more concerned with the socioeconomic issues plaguing the world—and that made her parents edgy.

'Were all the business families in their circle paying their workers minimum wage?'

'Were the most successful business tycoons funding the

politicians to bend policies in their favour?'

By the age of 12, these were questions that Maya posed casually to her parents' friends at Diwali card parties.

Mr and Mrs Khanna soon realized that Maya was too 'woke' for her own good—and this was long before the term even existed—Maya was a millennial, and the concept of being 'woke' wouldn't gain traction until years later. And so Maya's grooming began. To make her life even more luxurious, her parents set in motion a machinery to subtly influence her into thinking that she wanted to do something—anything— in fashion—so that she would keep it 'light' and not use her brains to tackle larger issues like poverty alleviation, which could invite controversy. After all, the Khannas lived to be the belles and beaus of the ball.

Mr Khanna expanded his pharmaceutical business into a luxury franchise empire so that he could secure Maya's interests there. While Maya wanted to dive deeper into developmental economics at the London School of Economics—a programme she had been accepted into— her parents gave her a gentle nudge towards what they thought would be more aligned with her interests and, ahem, probably their own—attending the London College of Fashion.

Maya got engaged to Samar on her 25th birthday. Her parents were thrilled that their princess had found a man worthy of being called a prince. Samar Singh hailed from one of India's biggest textile manufacturing families and was dubbed the 'Prince of Polyester'—by a publication Samar's father paid in the hopes of making the name stick. You see, there was only one thing more important to the Khannas and Singhs than the wealth they possessed: the perception of it. Thus, the union of Maya and Samar was viewed as a match made in ultra-high-net-worth heaven.

Despite the nagging thoughts of poverty and unemployment in her country that troubled her, Maya found ways to set them aside—by giving generous tips to the household staff, covering the college fees for their kids, or handing out wads of cash to roadside beggars. For the most part, Maya felt at peace.

Samar and Maya first met at a debutante ball in Paris, an exclusive event for children from elite families across the globe. He was handsome and kind, and made her laugh. They scoffed at the pretentiousness of the event and the caviar on their plate, later sneaking off to find *pani puri* in Paris. They ended the night watching *Kal Ho Naa Ho* in one of their suites at the Mandarin Oriental Hotel. Both seemed to wear the wealth and privilege they had been groomed into lightly and seemed to understand each other.

Maya had just returned from London after completing her master's in Luxury Brand Management, and the one year of long distance with Samar had only strengthened their bond. Now that she was back, after a quick trip to Italy, where she shopped until her wardrobe would put Kim Kardashian's to shame, Maya was ready to become Mrs Maya Khanna Singh. She was truly beginning to believe what everyone already thought of her—that she really had it all.

So days away from her birthday, things couldn't be better—at least from an outsider's perspective who aspired to such a lifestyle. Her father hinted at getting her dream car, her mother gifted her a year's supply of fillers for her already stunning face, and her long-time boyfriend, Delhi's most eligible bachelor, Samar, was about to propose. Once he completed his MBA at NYU Stern, they would have a big fat Delhi wedding, followed by a glamorous celebration for their friends in the south of France or Italy.

Samar and Maya were perfect on paper—the two most eligible kids from elite families in New Delhi were set to become one. Maya adored Samar's parents—heck, they were the most 'chilled-out' in-laws. Invitations for the engagement had already been designed by Samar's mother; the proposal was just a formality.

Everyone was guessing the carat size of Maya's engagement ring, with rumours swirling that Samar had shut down Tiffany's, just like Nick Jonas. Maya's Zuhair Murad gown from Paris lay carefully wrapped in French tissue, waiting to be worn on the big day.

Maya's birthday eve came, and so did a pink Porsche adorned with a golden bow in the driveway of their Malcha Marg residence.

She gave her parents a big hug and kiss before driving to Samar's home on Aurangzeb Lane. Her plans for the evening included a make-out session with Samar, a rerun of their favourite Shah Rukh Khan film and, of course, the proposal when Samar would go down on one knee. He could propose anywhere in the world, but she knew that they both shared the best memories in his room at home.

But when she arrived at Samar's house, instead of finding him on one knee, waiting for her, she was greeted by the sight of him in a downward dog position—naked—with a girl who looked familiar. Of course, this was Shanaya, the sultry, lean and tall woman with a horsey laugh who had been the subject of his Instagram stories—his new yoga teacher.

Maya felt like she had stepped on to the set of a reality show and was being punked—any moment the producers of the show would jump out and wipe away the tears that had started rolling down her cheeks faster than her Porsche had made its way out of her driveway to Samar's home. Surely, this was just Samar's last mean joke; she knew he could be a prankster sometimes. But as she stood there and nobody jumped out from the room, it became painfully clear that Samar and Shanaya were not actors playing a role but simply living their lives and going about their business.

Maya stormed out, racing down the never-ending spiral staircase of the Singh house, and zoomed out of the pristinely manicured driveway. Samar was cheating—not just with anyone but with a girl who was *way* beneath their social strata and lifestyle. This girl was from, *gasp*, Pune!

Devastated and heartbroken, Maya felt her life spiralling out of control. She knew that her once-perfect image—crucial for her parents and their business—was about to be shattered. The big fat Delhi engagement, which was set to be THE party of the season, would no longer happen. What face could she possibly show to anyone! And the worst part was that she had been hurt by someone she truly loved.

A week later, Samar arrived at the Khanna household with her favourite flowers—hydrangeas—flown in from London. Her parents had invited him to lunch. Maya resisted the urge, with every inch of her being, to not hurl the Lladró vase straight at his head.

In front of her parents, Samar asked Maya if they could

talk alone, leaving her with no option but to comply. She gave him three minutes to speak—the worst three minutes of her life.

No apology.

'You changed, Maya. We never took all this seriously,' he said, wagging his hands wildly like a shipwrecked man gasping for air. *The angry faces of the Souza paintings look like they want to eat him up,* thought Maya. She suddenly felt as pitiful as the G. Ravinder Reddy sculpture of a woman perched on their Italian dessert counter in the room—perfectly put together, obedient and wearing a resigned expression.

'So now you think I am too superficial, Samar?'

'Well, all you have talked about are your clothes for the summer and where you want to travel. What happened to "changing the world" and stuff like that we used to talk about? Striding into business and making our mark in the world with a bang?'

'Oh, so the skanky trainer girl from Pune you're banging is a yogi who wants to change the world and make it better one asana at a time by training her clients naked, right?' shot back Maya angrily.

She was about to storm out when Samar grasped her arms gently and pulled out a blue box from which something dazzled blindingly. It was the ring. As he held it out to her, Maya couldn't believe it. Did he really think things would just get okay?

She shook her head.

'You disgust me, Samar Singh. And speaking of business, your price equity ratio is way too high. It's only a matter of time before everything comes crashing down. But no free *gyaan* from me again. Do not call me or come here ever.'

Maya felt utterly devastated. She had actually loved this man. He knew everything she cared about, and now he was pretending she had no purpose! The luxury business had been thrust upon Maya much like his textile business had been thrust upon him. She knew she had the economic acumen and passion for fashion to make it work, but she had wanted more experience before stepping into that world, and Samar knew it. Yes, she talked about clothes all the time, but that was to distract herself from thinking about what lay ahead. She had wanted to work abroad before settling down with Samar in Delhi. Did that give him a free pass to go out and cheat—and that too on her birthday?

To make matters worse, every corner of Delhi reminded her of him—their favourite sushi place, the movie theatres, the coffee shops where they had savoured oatmeal lattes and even the parks where they had jogged together.

There was only one person who could make Maya feel better, but she wasn't there. In a frantic FaceTime with her best friend, who had just moved to the States, Natasha reminded Maya of her potential. 'You have always loved writing, ever since you were a little girl. And you always wanted to live in Istanbul. So why don't you apply for an internship in Turkey?'

Maya decided to pick up the pieces of her life. She would show the world, her parents, Samar, and all of Delhi just what she was truly capable of. Maybe Istanbul was just what she needed! It could be a chance to get over Samar and maintain a bit of a distance from her loving but overbearing parents.

Maya was determined—she would find a hot boyfriend to make Samar jealous, show him she could work to appeal to his newfound sapiosexual side and eventually, hopefully, make him regret what he had done.

But first, she needed a damn internship. She dove into her search and applied for two at *The Turkish Times*—one covering fashion and the other focusing on socioeconomic affairs.

She was offered both. The fashion internship started immediately, but socioeconomic reportage in Istanbul—a city that was a hotbed for such news—felt much more compelling. This was her chance to take risks.

On a whim and without consulting anybody, Maya booked tickets for Turkey and accepted the socioeconomic affairs beat. The tequila shots she downed at her gay best friend Jay's birthday solidified that decision in her mind. In just a week, she would be off to Istanbul, and now she had to break the news to everyone, mainly her parents. She was closest to her dad, so she decided to start with him.

Recovering from the initial shock, her dad wanted to know why she needed to cover socioeconomic affairs in Istanbul. 'Aren't there enough riots and *tamasha* in Delhi?'

She replied that it could have been worse—'It COULD have been Syria!'

There was another challenge—her mom believed that she would be pursuing the fashion internship, which sounded safer. Maya made her dad promise not to tell her mom the whole truth.

Giving up Samar—who was her parents' favourite—and leaving Delhi for Turkey was too much for the Khannas. They insisted she promise to FaceTime them twice a day and that this 'internship thing' would only be for three months, post which she HAD to come back to Delhi. Maya agreed, but these three months would be spent 'her way'. The Khannas agreed to the demands of their only child, albeit reluctantly.

Maya now made her way to a city that sounded dreamy but was, to her, totally alien and unpredictable—maybe like a hot stranger who could potentially be a closet serial sociopath... Okay, that was pushing it a bit far, but you get the drift. She landed in Istanbul nursing a broken heart but more determined than ever to mend it, and salvage her image and the remnants of her life in the process.

A week into her internship, reality hit Maya really hard. Her boss, the formidable Tatiania, was light on her feet but not on her employees. Maya had to report at 7 a.m. sharp every morning, including Saturdays. She also needed an appropriate wardrobe; one wasn't taken very seriously in haute couture at the serious *Turkish Times*.

Also, getting over Samar was proving just as difficult. Even small things, like baklava, triggered memories of Samar because that was his favourite dessert.

Back home, she had never needed to learn how to cook—her parents' house was staffed like a castle, after all. Her culinary expertise began and ended with cheese toast, which meant a lot of added carbs.

The first day, en route to work, Maya stumbled upon a small coffee shop near her apartment at Taksim Square. The waiter was SO cute, but wait... Would her parents approve of her dating a waiter? Indian parents often have a hierarchy of professions in mind, and the idea of a waiter as a potential partner would never ever be acceptable, even in a nightmare.

What would her snobby Delhi friends say? The cute waiter, Akser, who looked to be in his mid-20s, was a local boy with the most beautiful chocolate brown eyes and hair to match. He even offered her a free baklava with her coffee. Maya couldn't help but imagine him as the perfect candidate for a sweet Turkish romance, especially when their eyes met and he gave her a shy smile. Could there be something between them? Wasn't that the best way to get over Samar? *It's too soon, Maya,* she told herself. *Think with your head for once.*

She clicked a picture of herself, looking cute in a dress, stuffing her face with baklava, while Akser smiled in the background, blissfully unaware.

Maya uploaded the picture—#livingmybestlifeinTurkey.

She thought of her so-called friends back home who called up pretending to be sad for her when they found out about the broken engagement, only to dig deeper into the gossip. She thought of how Samar had dismissively told her that her conversations of late didn't match up to his needs and the fact that her love hadn't been enough for him. She remembered how, when making love, Samar would say, 'That was perfect,' and now Maya couldn't help but wonder if he had been fantasizing about that yoga teacher all along. He had the audacity to say she was too superficial for him. He wanted more—a girl with substance, a girl who could make a mark in the world. His words stung for days. 'All you care about are your clothes. What have you actually *done* with your life?'

Sitting in the café, Maya made a decision. She would be

open to all the possibilities this new city had to offer. And just for once, she would think only about herself and not worry about how her parents would feel.

She gobbled down the baklava, asked for the toilet to change into 'office attire' and ran to work. *Jesus. Instagram is a smokescreen.* But sometimes, that was exactly what one needed till the dust settled.

At *The Turkish Times*, her internship was proving to be far more challenging than she had anticipated. Working in the English edition, Maya quickly realized she was out of her depth. Tatiana was peeved that Maya didn't know even a little Turkish and made it clear that some knowledge of the language should have been a prerequisite. And then, the real bombshell dropped—Maya wasn't even supposed to be there. She had been mistaken for Mariam, a girl from Dubai who was actually supposed to be the intern. The mix-up had happened because of Tatiana's careless American secretary, Brad.

Brad was about 29, with a relaxed, almost careless, attitude towards work. He seemed determined to be Maya's friend. At first, she appreciated his efforts, thinking he was just being helpful, but then when he started leaving Turkish roses on her desk, she realized his interest extended beyond friendship. Just as Maya thought she had found a fellow out-of-towner to bond with, Brad's romantic overtures put her off. She started avoiding him and even turned him down when he invited her on a date—an evening cruise on the Bosphorus.

Meanwhile, Maya found herself increasingly drawn to Akser. She now woke up at the crack of dawn just to squeeze in 15 minutes of coffee time with him. The same routine unfolded each day—she would leave her apartment in a cute outfit, only to change into something more appropriate before heading for work.

Akser was dreamy, quiet and a great listener. Maya found herself telling him about her life in India. She told him about her childhood and dreams—maybe she could combine fashion and her socioeconomic interests and leave the luxury business to professionals. She did not talk about Samar, though.

Conversation flowed easily, and Maya opened up more and more to Akser. Samar used to listen to her too, but he would often interrupt. Akser, on the other hand, listened attentively and was easy-going.

At work, Tatiana paired Maya with Şevket, an established journalist, to mentor her. Şevket, in his 30s, was an experienced reporter from Istanbul who covered the toughest beats—from bomb scares to riots on Taksim Square. Maya was to shadow him, learn the ropes and report for the English edition of the paper.

One day, while shadowing Şevket during a bombing incident, Maya accidentally swiped 'accept' on an incoming video call from her mom. Maya had become good at making up stories on the fly. Quick on her feet, she concocted a story, telling her mother that it was part of Turkish festivities and the crowd had gathered for fireworks.

The last thing she needed was for her mom to find out she was reporting on bombings and riots instead of harmless fashion events. Her father, still in on the lie, kept her mom blissfully in the dark. So Maya sometimes showed up for work in colourful, trendy dresses and pantsuits—much to the bewilderment of Şevket. He probably thought it was absurd, her covering a bombing in Hermès wedges.

Şevket was a third-generation Turk from Persia. He was strong-willed, moralistic and dead serious about his job. But he also seemed to dislike Maya and snubbed all her suggestions and ideas, even ignoring her attempts at conversation.

Was Maya seriously going to be able to last like this, or would she end up going back to her embarrassing life in Delhi? The blind columns were already speculating why the 'First Lady of Luxury' didn't get engaged to the 'Prince of Polyester'. One article suggested that Samar hated her fillers—Maya hadn't gotten any yet and had told her mother she could use the gift instead. Another column speculated and got it right that Samar had cheated on her.

Maya tried to block out these noises that now seemed superficial. The more she covered her beat with Şevket, the more her old life felt like a fishbowl, where she had been trapped with other distracted and superficial beings.

Maybe Samar was voicing his own insecurities. After all, hadn't the textile empire been thrust upon him, regardless of whether he wanted to run it?

In the midst of challenging reportage, Maya would suddenly remember how irritable Samar could get after a seemingly fun evening. They'd have a great time at a party or dinner, but later, he'd snap at her, using the excuse of having to leave for NYU without her. *Snap back to Istanbul, Maya, and be present here like you promised yourself,* she would remind herself.

One beautiful evening, as the sun dipped behind a deep orange Bosphorus, Maya clicked a picture of herself against the backdrop of a serious protest. She was in her trendy clothes, just in case her mom called. She captioned the post #coveringstreetfashion #Turkishstyles and uploaded it as a story. Samar saw it within minutes. *Now he knows I have a trendy job.* She could have it all.

One for Maya. Zero for Samar.

He deserves that skank from Pune.

Just then, Şevket interrupted her triumphant mood. 'Is this how serious you are about what's happening?' he asked.

He was brooding more than usual. Şevket was tall, dark and always brooding. Every time Maya felt tempted to snap back, she held back because she needed this job more than it needed her. Besides, Şevket somehow became more attractive when he brooded, so Maya's anger would dissipate as quickly as it arose.

Meeting Akser at the café had become routine, but he still hadn't asked her out.

One evening—one of those rare evenings when she got off early after braving the wrath of Tatiana and the silent judgement of Şevket—Maya decided she needed a drink and headed to the café. She dressed up in her out-of-office attire, and, of course, Akser was there. The place was a little less boisterous than usual, and when Akser's shift ended, he joined her for a drink. They drank more than they should have, and before they knew it, they were back at her rented apartment. Maya had deliberately avoided staying at a lavish hotel lest her boss found out and fired her for not really needing this internship.

That night, it was like the stars had aligned... Even the leaky roof in the apartment behaved for a while. Akser and Maya kissed, and boy did sparks fly!

Maya fought the urge to unblock Samar even though she missed his voice. Instead, she curated her life on Instagram so that Samar would think she'd moved on and was living the best life.

Then, one day, Tatiana surprised her. 'You should go sightseeing if you want to understand Turkey better. You've earned it,' she said.

'That is the closest to a compliment from Tatiana one can hope for,' remarked Brad, who had overheard the remark.

Maya smiled politely at him. She and Brad barely talked these days since Maya spent a lot of her time shadowing Şevket on reportage.

So, on the one Sunday she had off, Maya decided she would go see the Hagia Sophia, and ask Akser if he would like to join her. After all, he had offered her a free cappuccino again just the day before, though he hadn't asked her out for a real date yet after their night together. As Maya reached the café, she spotted him and was about to walk up to him, when a drop-dead gorgeous girl kissed on the lips. Akser looked flustered but also comfortable. He pulled away but not till the kiss had lingered for a few seconds. *There goes your*

Turkish romance; you shouldn't have jumped into things so quickly and gotten carried away, she scolded herself quietly.

She turned to leave, but Akser had already seen her. He approached her and said, 'Hey, the other night was incredible,' looking deeply into Maya's eyes. 'I should have told you... That girl you just saw is my ex-girlfriend, Fatima. She just barged into the café to tell me how she loves me and wants to get married. She kissed me before I could even say a word!'

Maya's heart sank. This man had a gorgeous ex-girlfriend who was probably going to try and stay in the picture. *Guess I'll be touring the Hagia Sophia alone, and Samar will think I'm a loser... But did I really fall for Akser so quickly?*

This whole episode with Akser made Maya miss Samar and she unblocked him. As if on cue, her phone buzzed—Samar was calling. But Maya cut the call; she wasn't ready to hear what he needed to say just yet. Memories of him came rushing back—the time Samar asked her to be his girlfriend at his parents' anniversary party, the surprise Greek-themed 25th birthday party he had thrown for her, flying in Greek chefs and all. She sighed, snapping out of her reverie as her phone buzzed again. Another call from Samar.

She ignored it and a message popped up—'I am leaving for New York. Will be back in two months. Where are you? Your posts say Turkey. I hope you aren't doing anything stupid, Maya. I am sure this is hard for you... It is for me too. I spiralled. I am sorry I hurt you. I was a dick. It was last-minute jitters, and I shouldn't have blamed you. I am the biggest idiot.'

Maya read the text and then blocked Samar's number

again. She didn't want to hear anything from him for a while. Needing an escape, Maya headed to Sultanahmet Square alone. *What have I got to lose?* she thought as she joined a guided tour. She struck up a conversation with a British girl around her age. Maya couldn't help but notice her lime-green Sandro dress from the latest collection.

Rachel was a free-spirited fashion student from London studying in Istanbul. She was working on an assignment for class that day. She was also a part-time stylist and was invited to the best fashion events in town. Rachel and Maya hit it off right away. They decided to meet over drinks and discuss fashion. Maya realized that sometimes all one needs is a new friend in a strange land with a shared interest.

The next day at work Maya stumbled upon a feature story about none other than Akser. Turned out, Akser was one of the most eligible bachelors in Istanbul. His family owned a large chain of restaurants and hotels.

On Rachel's advice, Maya decided to speak to Akser openly. She could feel herself falling for him, especially after the heady hook-up. Akser came clean. He wanted to break up with Fatima for good, especially since meeting Maya, but it was complicated—the families wanted to form an alliance. Fatima's family owned a major media outlet, and the two families went back many years, just like Samar's and Maya's families.

She took two days off from work to process things. When Maya returned, things still felt heavy. But the terrifying Tatiana was in a rare good mood for a change.

Şevket was sulking, as usual, and left for a beat without Maya since she was now undergoing training on filing stories. Brad, who was once her informant on all things office gossip, barely spoke to her since she had turned down his advances. Left with no choice, Maya decided to go straight to the source and ask Tatiana why she was so thrilled.

Tatiana's sister had just gotten engaged. She even pulled out her phone to show Maya a picture of her sister. It was none other than Fatima. The engagement party was set for later that month, and nearly the entire office, including Şevket, Brad and Maya were invited!

Suddenly, Maya felt like she was nursing two heartbreaks. *But wait... What if Akser broke off the engagement like he really wanted to and asks me out? Tatiana would chew me alive and literally feed me to wild dogs on the outskirts of Istanbul.*

Maya's disturbing reverie was interrupted by a text from Şevket, who informed her that they had received assignments outside the Hagia Sophia for the following day. *Well, at least I'll get to see the Hagia Sophia again.*

※

Maya headed for her assignment with a heavy heart and a head full of confusion. She posted a picture of the Hagia Sophia on her Instagram feed. In it, the side profile of Şevket's head and his long neck were partly visible. She finished her assignment and headed home, grateful for the drama-free solace of her accommodation—aside from the leaky ceiling.

The next day, Maya woke up to find that her photo had gone viral. Turned out, Şevket was more famous than he let on; he was a highly respected reporter. Maya was suddenly impressed and felt grateful for the opportunity to work alongside someone like him.

Maya unblocked Samar again. As memories of their celebratory dinner after he got into NYU flashed through her mind—their friends toasting the perfect couple with #SaMaya—Maya read through a dozen messages he had sent. He had seen the viral photo and was now asking her who the mystery man was, while also apologizing profusely for cheating on her. *It took a mystery man for him to apologize to her this much?* Maya thought in disbelief.

Maya's mind briefly flashed back to a time when she had suspected Samar of hiding phone messages from her. *Snap back to the present, Maya.*

She finally replied to Samar, telling him that the man was her famous colleague and that she had landed her dream internship in Istanbul. She decided not to tell him about how Şevket was a difficult mentor and how he constantly snubbed her.

Deep down, Maya felt guilty that she was on Mariam's internship. Brad still hadn't realized the goof-up; if she pointed out now, they both stood to lose their jobs. Maya had only learnt about it when she got an email from the admin, addressing her as 'Mariam'; she had decided to keep the information to herself.

Then there was Akser. He had left her a note on her front door, claiming that he had called it off with Fatima and would like to take Maya out on a real date—a tour of beautiful Istanbul by foot.

Back at work, a new intern had joined—Mariam. The admin had realized the error and had finally sent her the letter. *Where will this leave me now?*

Şevket then surprised Maya by asking her to join him at a grand ball honouring journalists. 'After all, at least one of us will look fashionable. Maybe you can finally wear your couture where it's meant to be worn—in a ballroom,' he said in his usual brooding tone.

Maya decided to wear her Zuhair Murad gown. *Time to put it to good use.*

The next few days had Maya navigating the ups and downs of her internship, her budding attraction to Akser that now seemed complicated, the upcoming journalist ball with Şevket, and Brad's bizarre one-sided affection for her. But the real chaos was yet to begin.

One morning, Maya woke up to a flood of notifications on her phone. Her latest Instagram post, featuring a protest in the background with her casually posing in her Hermès wedges, had gone viral—but for all the wrong reasons.

The comments section was blowing up, not with praise for her trendy attire but with outrage. 'Out of touch!' one user screamed.

'Insensitive fashionista during a political crisis!' another wrote.

Maya's attempt to blend fashion with serious reporting had backfired spectacularly, and now she was being roasted on social media as 'The Unwoke Delhi Girl Interning in Istanbul' with comments branding her as 'a spoilt South Delhi girl out of touch with the world'.

Panicking, Maya scrolled through the comments only to

discover that someone had leaked an old photo of her with Samar at one of their lavish Delhi parties. The caption read, 'When your biggest crisis was choosing the right shade of lipstick for your Delhi wedding.' Ouch.

What made it worse was that the leak wasn't random—it was intentional. Maya's rise to online fame had been engineered by none other than Fatima, Akser's almost-ex-fiancée! Apparently, Fatima had used her family's media company's social media team to put her plan into action, aiming to destroy Maya's reputation now that she had discovered Akser's interest in Maya.

Maya found herself caught in the middle of a digital firestorm. But that wasn't the only bombshell. On the same day, during a chaotic morning meeting at *The Turkish Times*, Brad rushed in, breathless and pale. He had a confession to make—he wasn't just a clueless secretary with a crush—he was Tatiana's and Fatima's half-brother and an equal heir to their father's media empire.

Their father had sent him to work undercover in the newsroom to prove his worth as a journalist. He had only recently found out about Tatiana's involvement in Maya's 'accidental' internship placement. It turned out that Tatiana had deliberately hired Maya in place of Mariam—not out of carelessness, but to sabotage Brad's reputation in their father's eyes. Tatiana believed that creating chaos in political coverage would win her father's affection as she competed with Brad for the role of CEO, ever since he had come unexpectedly from the US. Maya had been a pawn in a much bigger scheme, but now, both she and Brad were caught in the crosshairs of Tatiana and Fatima.

Feeling cornered, Maya decided it was time to take control of the narrative. Instead of retreating into obscurity as she'd done after Samar, she leaned into the chaos. With Brad and Rachel by her side, she launched a full-fledged rebranding campaign. Maya Khanna 2.0 wasn't just a fashionista; she was a fierce social media strategist, using her newfound fame to build a platform that blended fashion and political commentary; her slogan—Knowledge and taking a stand are in Vogue. The beautiful landmarks of Istanbul became backdrops for stories about marginalized voices and pressing socioeconomic issues. She wore her couture clothes to gain traction because who says one can't care in couture?

To everyone's shock, Maya's rebranding caught fire. She became the poster child for unapologetically merging style with substance, transforming the backlash into her unique selling point. *The New York Times* took notice, declaring, 'This Indian girl is merging fashion with factual social commentary in Istanbul.'

Even Şevket looked proud of her. 'I have to admit, this mentor has learnt something from his protégée,' he announced, waving *The New York Times* article.

It had now been three months in Istanbul.

As the day of the gala arrived, Maya felt excited. Thoughts of Samar no longer haunted her. Her mother also now knew that she was not covering fashion events. 'I couldn't be prouder, beta,' her mother had said over a phone call.

The gala was a grand affair. Everyone was dressed to the nines.

But then Maya spotted two familiar faces, and one of them made her jaw drop. It was Samar. He walked towards her. 'I read *The New York Times* article. I had the weekend off and found out where you'd be tonight with a little help from your boss.' He glanced at Tatiana, who seemed engaged in a heated conversation with a fellow journalist from a competing media outlet.

Maya didn't know what to think. She felt numb. After missing Samar so much, his sudden appearance felt like an unwelcome commercial interrupting a gripping show. Just then, someone tapped her shoulder. It was Akser, looking more gorgeous than ever. 'I am sorry for what Fatima did to you. I really like you, Maya.'

At that moment, Samar went down on one knee, flipping open that blue box, which he had earlier brought to her home, and flashing that blinding diamond ring. The gesture seemed rushed and caricaturish, even though Maya was impressed by his audacity to propose at a random event.

'Maya, we need to be together,' he said quietly.

In front of a gasping audience, Maya faced two proposals—one from her past and one from her present.

'I've spent my whole life playing by other people's rules,' she addressed both men. 'Samar's, his parents', my parents' and even yours, Akser, in a way.' Maya then declared, 'But no more. From now on, I will write my own story. And right now, my story wants neither of you. Go back to New York, Samar. We both know we rushed this and now are salvaging this for our families. We may love each other, but we spoilt it by feeling the pressure to have the perfect proposal, engagement and wedding, just to appease our fishbowl society. And Akser, it's okay to take some time to really process what you're feeling because, let's face it, you did kiss Fatima back that day. So maybe she's not fully the villain here.'

With that, Maya made her way out of the gala into a silent drizzle. She texted Şevket that she would see him at work tomorrow, imagining his brooding look when he read that message, which made her smile. She wondered why Brad had missed the gala, and thought about what a good friend he had been. A text from Rachel popped up, inviting her to a college fashion show next week.

As Maya made her way to her leaky-roofed apartment, she looked forward to deep sleep after such an eventful and long evening. Maybe she'd stop by one of the cute little cafés on Taksim Square for baklava without worrying about whether her Zuhair Murad gown would feel tighter the next time she wore it.

Forbidden

When we fell in love in our third year at university, I realized that telling my father I was gay would be the easier part. The tougher part would be confessing that his son was, in fact, in love with a Muslim boy. Yep, that would be the toughest revelation, because now, being gay would come second to being with a Muslim, whether straight or gay. We will come to the reasons for this in some time, but that third year had me reflecting on my wonder years and strategizing how best to break the news to my father, that I had not only found the love of my life but was actually going to spend my life with him in what I was hoping would be matrimonial bliss.

My father had sensed me peeking out of the closet several times during my teenage years, yet why he chose to ignore it was known only to him. He was an extremely perceptive man and I always gave him the signs. Dad never asked too many questions, which, let's be honest, what teenager would complain about?

Take, for instance, my decision to skip prom night, a night every straight guy hoped to get 'lucky'. Instead, I stayed at Amit's because we had been working for weeks on a project that had to be submitted for, well, college applications. It helped that Amit owed no explanations to anyone because he lived with his octogenarian *daadi*, who was night-blind. Or consider my Sundays spent shopping for lingerie, saris or makeup with my mom instead of spending the afternoon sleeping in after a heavy night of beer and football like the other boys my age.

Then there was the day my dad found a size S boxer in the wash—one that belonged to no male in the household. It was from a one-night stand whom I had sneaked in through the main entrance while everyone, including Chotu, our house help, was asleep. Chotu seemed to notice everything, even with one eye shut, and reported everything to his sahab—my dad. Chotu sometimes gave me the side-eye, especially after I became more audacious, throwing caution to the wind as my hormones raged and my one-night stands became more frequent. He'd give me the unmistakable 'I have told Sahab' look, and I'd spend days on edge, waiting for Dad to bust me. But that moment never came. Eventually, I made peace with the fact that perhaps Dad had chosen denial, which suited me fine.

Now, going back to why being with a Muslim was forbidden. My father's generation had been children during the Partition, chased out of their homes on buses stripped of seats to cram as many as possible inside, like cattle, so they could cross the border to a new country where they would have to start from scratch. Religious lines were drawn across what was once a single nation, now split into two. They left behind not only livelihoods but everything and everyone that defined them. My grandfather's sister died during childbirth at the young age of 23, on the eve of

Partition. Her body couldn't be cremated because riots were raging outside. And if that wasn't enough, from an unknown window in a stranger's home—who had been kind enough to take the family in—my father, just seven years old, witnessed men slaughtering one another in the deadliest and bloodiest riots in the name of religion.

While those experiences spurred him to become a stellar businessman, they also ensured he never forgot that his aunt couldn't be cremated, that his cousin was born an orphan and that 'his Hindu people' had their heads severed and hearts stabbed for worshipping different gods.

But that time had come to pass. Cut to the present: Gen Z is doing absurd things, and even eight-year-olds are referring to themselves as 'they/them', something I know my boomer father is struggling to wrap his head around. My father is progressive overall, so I figured I could ease the whole 'Muslim' thing into the conversation when I came out and introduced Amaan at the same time. I thought it would go something like this: during the upcoming holidays, when I was back in Delhi, I would have Amaan over for dinner for our Thursday biryani night—when Dad is always in a cheerful mood. I would start by telling him about my stellar grades—first-class honours in Economics and a job as an analyst at a major consulting company in London. Then, after the ice had been broken and a glass or two of wine had been enjoyed, I would slowly let slip that Amaan wasn't my best bro, as I had been referring to him all along, but in fact, my best bae.

Dad would guffaw. *'Ab ye "bae" kya hai, abbe?'*—'Now what is this "bae", son?'—he'd say, before launching into his trademark, infectious laugh.

Then, after the lamb biryani had been devoured and had settled warmly in our bellies, I'd go in for the kill. 'Dad, Amaan Ali is my bae—before everyone else. The *one*. You always knew, didn't you?... That...well...I am not straight... And now that I am settling into work, what better time to tell you?'

So, you see, the Amaan Ali bit would just slip in, like a well-executed tennis backhand—like those matches Dad loves watching. He'd put me in tennis classes to try and make me play for the state, because, well, a 'true man' always excels at a sport, just like Dad excelled at table tennis till the state level.

Honestly, in this day and age, it should be a celebration that I at least identify as something—like Mr Gay. Dad had already expressed his frustration when he had to interview someone who asked to be referred to as 'they/them'. The HR manager had been given a good bellowing: 'I don't care if it's GEN Z or GEN D. If someone cannot decide whether he is he or she is a she, he/she cannot work in my company.' No one dared tell Dad—not least the poor HR manager—that if he said this out aloud a few more times, he would be cancelled, and his company's shares on the stock market would plummet.

Dad belonged to an entirely different generation—a generation of boomers, who at the age of seven were trying to hide from riots and, hence, didn't have the privilege to decide which pronoun they wanted to identify with. Their parents were too busy trying to light a fire and keep a roof over their heads after losing everything to a political decision that they had had no say in.

So yes, Dad's attitude came more from a place of genuine ignorance than from a lack of empathy. In fact my father was incredibly empathetic. His employees adored him, and he treated them well. Correction: his gender-binary employees loved him. As for the rest, they might have been tiptoeing out of closets and tool rooms just to stay in his good graces.

If the dinner had gone according to plan, Dad might have been momentarily speechless, while Mom would have cracked a witty joke with her effortless candour (it helped that she had known for ages). The moment would pass, never to be spoken of again, and the ALI part of it would be quietly swept under the rug—at least until the morning, when I would present Dad with the wedding card. That had been the plan all along.

But who knew that the love of my life, my bae, Mr Amaan Ali, had plans of his own that preceded our gala wedding plans!

I almost choked on my avocado sandwich when he announced it. We were at that new café just outside uni, White Lily, just off Marylebone Lane. They had the best oat milk latte, and it helped that they refilled my steel water bottle as many times as I wanted—because, well, I was feeling the pinch of spending in pounds, with inflation skyrocketing. The UK's first Indian PM seemed to be doing nothing to control rising prices or the wave of muggings, and was definitely embarrassing his father-in-law, a first-generation entrepreneur who clearly knew how to manage costs and had built a multi-billion company from scratch.

'You want me to what?' I sputtered. 'You mean you want me to convert the euros that you have saved into pounds, right? Because surely we are not talking about any other conversion!'

And that's when Amaan Ali, the love of my life, ceased to look like Amaan Ali, my bae, but became an entirely different entity altogether.

It turned out Amaan had broken the news about me to his dad the night before. Yes, it helped that his dad knew he was gay. No, it didn't that he didn't know that I was Hindu. Amaan's father was a leader of a political party diametrically opposite to the one my father supported. If there was to be any union, his strict order was that I would have to convert. 'And what did you say to that?' I asked, taking a big gulp of my oat milk latte. Amaan's puppy eyes answered before he could. He had said nothing. No revolt. No argument. It was almost as though the Amaan I fell in love with while drinking wine and discussing Sartre's existentialism had ceased to exist.

'Well, if you had told me "no wine at the wedding" for your teetotaller family's sake, that would have been a bigger let-down,' I joked, hoping Amaan would say that this was an April Fools' prank, albeit a week late. But no. It was 7 April, and it was too late for jokes. This was serious. And I remember that date because it was the last time I saw Amaan at White Lily. In fact, it was the last time I saw Amaan, ever.

Right after this announcement, he walked off, almost like an alien returning to his planet. Despite my repeated messages asking him to try and find a middle ground, he said he just couldn't fight with his dad. Besides, the conversion would only be symbolic—who cared!

I did. And I know this was one thing I couldn't hide from

my father, who had seen enough in his lifetime. The biryani dinner happened, but without Amaan. The coming-out happened, but without Amaan. I even confessed to my father about Amaan Ali and everything that had transpired.

With tears welling up in his large, all-knowing eyes, he said, 'Well, puttar, if this is really what you want, go ahead.'

But by then I had realized that if I needed to change my identity, even 'just symbolically' for my bae, my heart had already cancelled out such love... Because the love for my identity was stronger. Love should never hinge on what you identify with—religiously or otherwise.

Amaan did get married...to a girl. Political pressure from his father. I am sure he lives a dual life to preserve his sanity. I did find love again. While I believe in God, my new partner doesn't. And that hasn't been a point of contention till now. We plan to make our union official by marrying with the blessings of both our parents. I do miss Amaan and we send each other the occasional 'Happy Diwali' and 'Happy Eid' messages. I hope he is happy.

Elite Club

She held on to her virginity for a very long time, as if it were a lifetime membership of a supremely exclusive elite club. But when the cherry finally popped, it didn't feel like anything special; in fact, it was an anticlimax before she could even climax (no pun intended). Almost immediately, she began to regret the membership she had finally relinquished on her wedding night, her *suhag raat*.

Pia was an '80s kid—1989, to be precise. A millennial. Her seven-year-old self used to be buried in a Roald Dahl chocolate factory or busy solving a *Secret Seven* mystery—as opposed to the Gen Zs now, who are preoccupied with their pronouns and gender identity—having no idea what 'millennial' meant.

She understood it but didn't really get it. They/them/theirs... Was expanding one's identity more important than expanding one's vocabulary?

Her marriage of six years was stable but stale, much like some of the chocolate fondue cakes at her confectionery—people wanted gluten-free these days, but Pia was a sucker for old-school desserts and reluctant to introduce any of the 'modern stuff'.

She and her husband, Zee, had talked about having kids,

but she was desperate to make some headway in her baking business. Pia's dream was to open a bakery in every major city across the country. Yet, here she was, struggling to sell cakes from just one bakery, nestled in a busy shopping area of her city, Delhi. The rent for the space was soaring and Zee, whose start-up was in its second year of double-digit PAT (profit after tax), was covering three-quarters of it. Was it the insecurity of never making it? The nagging feeling of failure? The desire to have it all—a perfect marriage and a thriving career—or the capriciousness she had allowed to seep into all her relationships that made her so combustible? She felt like an old kettle set to boil over, teetering on the edge, whether dealing with her employees at work or with Zee at home.

Pia couldn't pinpoint it to one single cause. But when she looked back at the day she met *him*, she realized she had already been at her tipping point.

It began on an otherwise mundane day. A man walked into her bakery to buy pastries. He had a chocolate-brown complexion, a well-built frame with a flat torso and eyes that smiled even when his face remained stoically calm. Perhaps it was that calmness she longed to dive deep into because her life of late had felt like a turbulent flight with an unreliable pilot—her.

His name was Raj, and he wore a steel wedding band, very similar to the one she had given Zee on their engagement. What stood out was how Zee always wore his, even through their worst arguments, and even when they threw around the word 'divorce' like a dagger.

Yes, they had gone there—not once, but multiple times.

Zee had become distant when alone with her, condescending in front of his family and friends, and outright dismissive in front of her parents. He wasn't the sweet, kind Zee she knew once. But then, again, she wasn't the dependable, affectionate and caring Pia she once had been either.

Raj ordered her favourite—a box of chocolate éclairs with a cream filling—and asked for a card. She caught a glimpse of his neat cursive handwriting as he scribbled 'To my sweet love'.

While paying, he gave the cashier a small wink (which Pia noticed from her office) and said, 'This is for my fiancée,' with a harmless audacity that made her want to speak to him. It didn't hurt that he looked good as well.

Every fibre of Pia's being wanted to rush out from her corner office to the cash counter, but she remained rooted to the spot. She knew she wasn't much of a flirt. Sharp, petite and attractive with full lips that occasionally spewed some wise and witty lines, she had never been a flirter, the one to initiate flirting. She had always been the *flirtee*, the one who got flirted with. So her flirting game sucked and, besides, what would it lead to anyway?

The second time they crossed paths was at the opening of a mutual friend's restaurant. Pia had begged Zee to come along, but he had been growing more and more socially reclusive. She couldn't stomach another evening at home discussing finances, buying a house (they were still renting, and the skyrocketing rent meant they were left with zero savings), children (he wanted them; she did too—just not yet) and his, *erm*, sex drive.

So she made it a point to go out more frequently to escape the looming thorns in their shared life.

And there was Raj, this time with his fiancée. As Pia hung out with her and Zee's friends, she ended up exchanging a look with Raj. His eyes smiled while his face remained stoic and calm, as it had at the bakery. She found herself wondering if that was genuine or if he was simply adept at playing charming tricks.

They quite literally bumped into each other outside the powder room.

'Oh, I am so sorry,' said Raj.

Pia caught a whiff of his cologne—vanilla and walnut—very fresh. The space was a 1920s-inspired Art Deco speakeasy, with the bathroom door framed by a stained-glass mirror that reflected their faces with an Instagram-like 'faded warm' filter. Pia suddenly felt the urge to apply lipstick.

'How were the éclairs?' she asked impulsively, startling herself.

It was one of her many self-sabotaging tendencies—starting conversations at the wrong time, in the most inappropriate places. This, was why she rarely was the flirter.

Great, Pia. Now explain how you know that.

'The éclairs... Rose Bakery. I was there that day,' she wanted to say, but no words came out.

'Wait, are you stalking me?' Raj laughed, his stoic face finally breaking into a broad smile.

'I'm kidding,' he quickly added, 'and if you *are* stalking me, it must be my lucky week.' With a wink, he disappeared.

Pia let out a laugh—one that lit up her eyes—and walked into the powder room. She felt excited about someone or something—an emotion that had been eluding her for months.

※

The third time she ran into Raj was at a funeral. A common friend's aunt had passed away. This time, the fiancée was missing. Raj was standing outside, lighting a cigarette, while Pia had stepped out to take a call—her father, calling about her tax returns.

'What do you even say at these things?' Raj asked, exhaling a smoke ring into the air.

'Dad, I'll call you back!' Pia whispered into the phone.

'I mean, I just heard an aunty discussing everyone's white outfits and deciding that cream looks better than stark white for such occasions,' continued Raj. His expression remained stoic, though his voice carried a tinge of amusement.

'And then that aunty went ahead and clicked a picture in her white kurta and *juttis*. I bet she Instagrammed it!' He stubbed out his cigarette with a tap of his ice-blue shoes.

'We would have lost the popular vote,' Pia replied, eyeing Raj's blue linen T-shirt and torn denim jeans, and her own pastel yellow salwar kameez with mild deliberation.

'Yeah, we totally would have!' Raj grinned this time, his face finally matching the smile in his eyes. Pia felt a blush rise to her cheeks.

She had rushed from the bakery as soon as she had heard about Kamala Aunty's passing and hadn't had the time to change her clothes.

Kamala Aunty had been a loyal patron of Rose Bakery. She always came in with a jovial energy and left imparting some life lessons that almost always involved the word 'principles'. She had a habit of mixing up phrases, in the most endearing way. Just last week Kamala Aunty had stopped by to buy some macaroons, and while paying, she had said, 'Bacche, hard work is worship! Must live by such principles.'

The new 20-something cashier from the Northeast hadn't seemed to notice, but Pia had. She now realized that that was going to be the last lesson she would ever hear from Kamala Aunty, and a pit formed in her stomach.

In a world that moved so fast—one-click deliveries, blink-and-you-miss-it social media likes and transient spaces that are here today gone tomorrow—customers like Kamala Aunty offered her a sense of stability. No matter what changed, Kamala Aunty's cake order and mixed-up life lessons remained a constant, and Pia had found a strange solace in that.

'So, how did you know Kam Aunty?' asked Raj, looking genuinely interested.

'Well, she was my school friend Natasha's *masi*, and a regular at my boulangerie.' Pia had meant to say 'bakery' but she sometimes slipped into French when nervous. Also, it was amusing when people didn't get it and asked her to translate.

'Oh, I didn't know you owned a bakery. Oh, of course— Rose is yours!' Raj exclaimed, as if he had just discovered she was a NASA scientist.

'I wouldn't expect you to know anything about me. We don't know each other!' Pia replied, a bit too quickly. She realized her words had come out wrong—too haughty, even though that hadn't been her intention.

'Why? I would expect anyone to want to know everything about someone like you,' said Raj, his smiling eyes piercing right into hers.

Just then, her phone rang. It was Zee. She quickly cut the call, hoping Raj hadn't noticed. But then Raj's phone rang.

'Hey, babe... Yes, I met Natasha. I told her you were under the weather... I'll see you soon. Love you.'

The voice on the other side sounded spontaneous—too spontaneous for Pia's liking. They were standing close enough for her to overhear every word.

'Was that who the éclairs were for?'

'Oh, so you like to beat people in their own game—wanting to know everything about them before they even have a chance to ask your name?' Raj teased, his voice sweet but with a slight cockiness that Pia found hot. She felt herself blushing again.

'It's Pia,' she said, extending her hand, feeling oddly formal.

Raj took her hand in his, and they both held on for longer than necessary. He pulled his hand away and said, 'Hey, give me your number. The éclairs were just too good, but I'll need a direct line to complain when they aren't an 11/10—if that situation ever arises.'

Pia couldn't help but smile, feeling her face flush even more. She looked away as she recited her number.

'Oh, and I know Kam Aunty because she was my godmother. And what a freaking godmother she was. I guess

God needs people like her close by. I feel semi-abandoned, honestly... And really, this is what counts, right?' he said, pointing to his chest. 'What's in here, not appearances. But, boy, am I glad I didn't show up in cream!'

And with that, he walked away, leaving Pia transfixed and totally unaware that she had missed four more calls—two from her father and two from Zee.

Whenever Pia reminded Raj of that day, and the first two times they had met, he just wouldn't admit he was the one who had started flirting. But then, again, they never admitted to anything. They never even acknowledged that this was becoming a thing, even after texting each other every day for a month, exchanging countless odd messages.

Pia noticed that her squabbles with Zee had lessened since her texting exchanges with Raj began. She had initiated them by sending 'I hope the last batch of éclairs met your approval, or we can totally refund your money!' It hadn't been a spur-of-the-moment idea, but a fully thought-out one.

Pia had texted exactly five days after meeting him at the funeral. This was her first attempt at flirting with any man since getting married. Why couldn't she text a prospective customer or friend? Deep down, she knew he was going to be neither, but she used that as her alibi to appease the 'good girl' voice of her conscience—the only one she was willing to acknowledge at the time. Pia was the kind of person who believed in remaining loyal to a skincare brand for eternity, even if it gave her acne now and then. She simply was that person. So deliberately wanting something outside of her marriage—let's just say she wouldn't entertain that thought, even in her wildest fantasies.

But Pia didn't believe in anything that might be labelled as the wild side of things. Besides, it really was Zee she wanted, both physically and intellectually. A different story that the compatibility in those areas was waning, but Pia would never stop trying. Commitment and monogamy meant everything to her.

When she sent that text, she had no idea whether Raj had even ordered éclairs. But she thought the message was just the right balance of cheeky, cute and confident. Maybe if she had paused to reflect on how she was sounding, just maybe she could have stopped what was about to become a roller coaster of emotions in the days to come—a roller coaster of emotions for someone whose existence she had been unaware of till a few days back.

Pia and Raj messaged about frivolous stuff, world events, work (Raj was an investment banker—who would have guessed!), their favourite movies, travel, food, desserts—but they never spoke about their respective relationships. Not one exchange. She didn't ask him about his fiancée, when their D-day was, and he never enquired about her marital status.

Once she told him how whenever she gave her name for restaurant bookings as 'Mrs', people would do a double take and then comment on how she looked too young to be married, whatever that meant. To that, Raj had responded, 'Coming from a country where they wed you in your nappies, you look pretty old, bruh!'

Pia had laughed at that. She liked that he had a sense of humour and that he never asked for details, not even the name of her husband.

Then she got pregnant. And suddenly, she didn't feel like herself any more. She told Raj about it and then stepped out of her comfort zone by asking to meet him. She said she needed to 'discuss' how she felt about having a baby with someone who wasn't going to have any direct connection with it.

Raj joked, 'I would have asked if it was mine, but—oh, fuck—we never got the chance, did we? Maybe in our next lives?'

Pia knew they now had such an equation that he could say something like that.

They met at a coffee shop. She wasn't expecting to cry, but the tears came anyway. And then it all got too much and Raj offered to drop her home. On the way, Pia told him to take a longer route.

'I feel guilty I don't match up to Zee's excitement about the baby,' she admitted. By then, Raj understood Zee was her husband's name, though it had never been mentioned before.

'Oh, that happens all the time. Sam gets excited about almost everything, and sometimes you just fake it so you don't let your other half down. Come on, life could be worse. You could be faking an orgasm all your life. I'd rather choose faking excitement over some news. Besides, maybe I am too much of an existentialist to ever really be excited about anything, and that could be hard for anyone to deal with.'

Pia wasn't sure what it was about their time together that evening, but she knew she didn't want it to end.

'Can we get another cup of coffee somewhere else? Maybe at your place? Besides, I really need to see just how geeky this outhouse of yours is.'

Raj had often talked about how he spent most of his time after work in an outhouse. He described it as a modern, fully functional cottage near his family's bungalow. He joked that he only went to the main bungalow to sleep because, in his words, he was 'basically scared and a baby like that'.

The rain came down hard as they entered the main gates. Pia found the outhouse to be more modern and uber-cool than the 'geeky' hideout she'd imagined.

Raj was a comic-book geek and had a huge collection, along with LDs and DVDs.

'Should we watch a film?' Pia asked.

'Yeah! Let's finally watch *Notting Hill*.'

It was a movie they had discussed at length during their text exchanges. Fifteen minutes into the film, the rain began to pour even harder. The outhouse door rattled and Pia instinctively reached out for Raj's hand. This time they let their touch linger in contact, neither of them pulling away. Before they knew it, they were undressing each other.

Sex with Raj was amazing—but not in the same way it was with Zee. With Zee, it was technically perfect. But with Raj, Pia felt certain that their bodies had united this way in some previous life.

'Are you hungry?' asked Raj. 'I can ask Chotu to get those burgers I keep telling you about!'

Pia noticed his phone vibrating silently, Sam's name flashing on the screen. Raj pretended not to notice.

'I think I better get going before...before...this turns into a real crisis,' said Pia. She didn't know what else to say.

Raj had *Red Hot Chilli Peppers* on full blast in his car when he dropped her home. Pia had already rehearsed her alibi—if Zee asked, she'd say she had been in a work meeting with a potential investor, an investment banker who knew people who might want to invest in her bakery and had dropped her home since her driver was on leave. Pia had deliberately chosen a day the driver was on leave. It just felt more private that way, especially because her driver kept a mental note of everywhere she went. She hadn't planned to sleep with Raj that evening. Maybe the thought had crossed her mind, but only fleetingly.

After that day, their messages to each other grew more urgent. *When was Raj getting married? What was Pia's due date?* Raj was getting married a year to the day he had proposed. As it turned out, Raj's wedding day and Pia's due date were just days apart.

'Wild!' commented Raj, but they never discussed that night. Instead, they talked about the meaning of life. Raj tried to keep the tone light but Pia knew he wasn't feeling frivolous; neither was she.

Pia's labour was long. She named him Jay, which meant victory.

She sent his pictures to Raj, who thought the baby was adorable. Zee was over the moon but also extremely paranoid about the baby's routine and everything. With Zee and her own family hovering because they all wanted to be around the baby, Pia felt like disappearing.

Raj got married a week later. The wedding was a two-day affair in Goa, followed by a month-long honeymoon in Europe. Their messages became infrequent and then suddenly stopped altogether, for two long months. Those were the longest months of Pia's life—filled with sleepless nights, aching joints, mood swings and another life to take care of all the time.

Oh, how she needed to talk to Raj!

And then Raj finally messaged, 'Hey! How are you and my little buddy Jay? Sorry, man, we stayed for another month and I couldn't text you.'

By then, Pia was finally getting a few hours of sleep, and she was tired—tired of missing Raj, more tired of not being able to tell him she missed him, tired of wondering if he was dead or alive (he wasn't on Instagram), apart from all the other tiring stuff that was going on in her life.

Pia pressed block.

He came to the bakery a month and a half after she had blocked him. It had been only a few days since she had returned to work, and business was slow. As Raj walked in, she ushered him into the back office. She often had meetings there, so it all appeared normal.

And that's when he confessed he was in love with her.

She was in love with him too... But things were going so well with Zee. Raj and Sam too were enjoying married life, apart from the deep pangs of longing he felt for Pia. He told her that he had thought of her a lot during those two months in Europe—on his honeymoon.

Then came the shocker.

'I have been offered a job at the Paris branch of my bank. Would you and Jay relocate with me? Hey, I am serious about us. If I have to call my marriage off sooner than Kim K did her first one, so be it. I care deeply about Sam, but I love you. You are my soulmate.'

Pia couldn't believe what she was hearing. From never even admitting to each other about their 'indiscretion', to suddenly this? Of course, she refused. Even if she were to entertain such a thought and hypothetically end it with Zee, her father would definitely have a heart attack from the shock. Her family was progressive but conventional—she could never do that to her father. And she wouldn't betray Zee like that. She loved him. If she loved Raj, she also truly loved and cared about Zee, despite the numerous pitfalls in their marriage. She could never hurt Zee to that extent.

Pia and Raj didn't speak again for three years until they bumped into each other at an art opening at Bikaner House. The artist was a mutual favourite. This time, Sam was pregnant, and Zee was working late, so both were absent. Besides, neither of them were fans of art exhibitions.

They went for a coffee at a small newly opened bistro nearby. Pia noticed strands of silver in Raj's otherwise shiny black hair. He smelled the same—walnut and vanilla—and had the same cocky smile in his eyes, with a calmness in his aura. They picked up from where they left off.

'You started it,' said Pia, when the topic of 'them' came up.

Raj tried to deny it, laughing. Raj and Sam had moved to Paris for a year but Sam hated living in a European city that frowned on the English language. Pia thought how, if she had been in Sam's shoes, she would have leapt at the chance to relocate. Then she remembered how Raj had asked her and Jay to come with him and felt a deep pang inside—the drop in the stomach one feels while on a roller coaster.

They talked non-stop, about how Raj and Sam would be moving to New York soon, how Pia and Zee had finally saved enough for the down payment on their dream house and how Jay was growing naughtier by the day, but had brought Pia and Zee closer than ever before. For the better, Pia thought.

After two hours of catching up, Pia asked if Raj would drop her home. As they settled inside Raj's car, they shared a deep, passionate, unexpected kiss. For some reason, Pia thought of the West End plays she enjoyed during her visits to London; the moment felt like the final act of a theatrical performance, just before the curtains fell.

They promised each other they wouldn't be in touch again.

'No rabbit hole of messages,' Pia insisted.

'Oh, I agree!' replied Raj.

With that, they decided never to contact one another again, and remained blocked on each other's phones and social media—until, of course, life decided to throw them back into each other's paths.

The Banker Cabby

Sujoy tapped his foot on the accelerator of his stationary black Mercedes outside the Four Seasons in Mayfair, where, in better times, clients had treated him to caviar and French wine over numerous meetings. It had been only a month since he had been the vice president of the Private Wealth Division at Barney's Bank, yet it already felt like an eternity since he last held the position. But then, this did feel like the longest month of his life. The shock of being fired after serving the bank for 20 years had been all too consuming.

Maya clunked the lock shut on her third suitcase, letting out a sigh of relief; she had been anxious that all her new shopping wouldn't fit. Her phone buzzed from her new Fendi bag, a reminder from the Uber app that it was time to head home. With a heavy heart, she glanced out of the window of the Four Seasons, her haven for the past month. The view of the hotel porch, where fancy cars pulled up carrying stylish guests and where immaculately suited staff greeted the visitors, had provided her with entertainment on many mornings while she sipped her 'room service' iced latte. She spotted a green

Lamborghini and a black Mercedes S-Class. She presumed the latter was her ride.

※

A sudden thump on the door startled him. He saw a pretty young girl with hazel eyes standing outside his car, looking impatient. Sujoy rolled down his window and greeted her. 'Hello, madam. Those look heavy!'

He stumbled out and grabbed one of the larger suitcases, which was heavier than he had expected. After tossing in the rest of her luggage, he noticed that she had settled in the back seat, engrossed in her phone.

Sujoy got into the car and started driving. He glanced in the rear-view mirror; the girl was gazing out of the window, looking wistful. *Those eyes*, he mused. He had known only two others with such deep-set hazel eyes, and that was a lifetime ago.

'So, how did you become a cabby?' she asked, catching him off guard. Sujoy hadn't expected that question. It still hadn't sunk in. 'Is it something you always wanted to do? Do you love driving? she continued her innocent enquiry.

After a moment of awkward silence, Sujoy finally found his voice. 'If that had been the case, madam, I would have become a Formula One racer,' he joked, attempting to maintain his usual wit. 'Nobody ever wants to become a cabby, madam. I was a banker once.'

Maya's eyes widened; she loved conversations with strangers. In New Delhi, her home town in India, everyone from her social circle seemed to know everyone else. You always encountered familiar faces at the usual haunts—the gym, the salon, your favourite restaurant or even that late-night cinema. Where was the excitement in that? They chatted about the same old topics—the latest soirée or the most recent social event.

She studied the stranger in front of her. He was well built, with thick black hair and a strong jawline. His black linen Massimo Dutti suit reminded her of something her father would wear to business meetings. He did appear to be around her father's age.

'You look too suave to be a taxi driver; that suit is from this year's spring–summer collection,' she said, a blush creeping across her cheeks as she realized how direct her words sounded.

'Wow, Madam! You really know your fashion! So, are you from London?' enquired Sujoy in an attempt to divert the attention away from himself.

'I am from New Delhi. I come to London every year; it's my family's favourite vacation spot. They had to leave earlier since my dad had work, but I decided to stay on for a few more days. I will join my dad's business once I am back in India,' Maya said. 'I completed my MBA a few months ago, and now it's time to take the plunge in the workforce.'

'And what is it you will be doing with him, if you don't mind me asking?'

'Manufacturing soap. That's our family business.'

Sujoy glanced in the rear-view mirror again. The girl's hazel eyes still searched for an unknown horizon outside. 'And is that what you dreamt of doing as a little girl?' The words escaped him before he could stop them. He realized he sounded overly inquisitive—an unwelcome trait in his new role as a taxi driver. He was still adjusting to the ins and outs of this job, having been accustomed to the respect that came with being a banker. If he were still in that role, no one would have minded his questions; in fact, his junior employees used to be thrilled when he gave them the time of day to discuss their ambitions. But it had all changed now. He was in a different kind of service sector, and this young lady had no obligation to engage in small talk. Perhaps it was even against protocol. *You need to talk less, Sujoy,* he reminded himself.

'Nobody asks me that,' Maya said with a grin. 'Well, I love fashion, but nowadays every other person is a fashion blogger. For me, it's more like loving to eat good food without wanting to run a restaurant. Yes, that's my relationship with fashion,' she mused. 'It would take the fun out of it if it became a job.'

'Numbers make me feel that way. I love them. Ironically, my previous job made them even more exciting,' Sujoy replied, nostalgia lacing his voice.

'So, what happened to your banking job?'

'I was laid off.'

'Oh... Why? Did the bank go bust?'

'No, it—'

'Oh my God, was it the "Barney's Bank Sack"?' she interjected, her eyes wide with recognition. 'I've been reading about it in the *Evening Standard*. They fired some important...' Her voice trailed off as she realized how insensitive she sounded.

'You are bang on,' Sujoy confirmed, affecting a blasé tone.

It suddenly hit Maya that this man was one of the top three people at Barney's Bank who had been fired on speculation of committing fraud. At least that's what all the newspapers had hinted at. Suddenly, the cab ride felt like a big adventure! *One of the most powerful figures in the banking world is now my cabby! Wow*! thought Maya. *But you mustn't pry,* she reminded herself.

Sujoy felt a blush creep up his cheeks. He wasn't ready to talk about it, not even with a stranger. When Jon, the president of the Investment Wing, had approached him with the plan, it had seemed fairly straightforward and foolproof. After all, they'd only intended to siphon off £50,000—not much in the grand scheme of things for the bank. They would subtly manipulate one fund that 50 of Sujoy's high-net-worth clients had invested in; each client losing a mere £1,000—negligible compared to the six-figure sums in their accounts. That's how Sujoy justified it to himself, thinking the substantial gains he had already delivered these clients in their other investments would offset this minor loss. He and Jon had been sure they would get away with it.

But someone had caught a whiff of their plan. Evidence emerged in the form of a recording from one of their covert meetings in Jon's cabin. The whistle-blower was a management trainee in Sujoy's team, who had presented the audio clip during the annual board meeting. Sujoy never saw it coming. He had always felt invincible, that no one could touch him. The harsh confrontation with the directors and his subsequent firing had shattered that illusion, cutting into him like shards of glass. He had been an idiot. In hindsight, he knew it wasn't the greed that drove him; he made more than enough money. He had done it for the thrill. *Maybe this was a midlife crisis. Middle age makes you do absolutely absurd, irrational things,* he thought. He deserved far more punishment than he had received. But the Barney's Bank board wanted to save face and had opted for a quiet dismissal. Of course, tabloids still got wind and were now abuzz with rumours and speculation, even after a month.

Sujoy considered himself lucky. The bank asked him to pay a fine to cover the damages he had caused. His reputation, or at least a part of it, was bruised but not entirely ruined. It had cost him nearly everything—his savings were almost depleted, leaving him with only his car and the prospect of starting over. Ironically, after years of advising others to invest their money wisely, he had never bothered with it himself. Perhaps it was the occupational hazard of talking endlessly about 'smart investing' that made him indifferent when his workday ended.

Was he remorseful about what had transpired? Yes. In his 20 years at the bank, he had never made a single penny through unethical means. In a way he was glad that he had been caught before he could. He remembered his first day at Barney's as a fresh-faced intern—the 'Cool Cambridge Boy' they had called him. *Thank God Baba isn't alive to see this*, he thought.

He noticed his passenger's curious expression. 'You got it right, Madam. I was part of the "Barney's Bank Sack". My name is Sujoy Ghosh, and you may have read about me in the papers.' He felt a flush of awkwardness, realizing just then that he had become infamous. Barney's had done its best to keep the information under wraps, but even walls have ears. And they were living in the age of instant information.

'There are two sides to every story,' Maya said unexpectedly. 'And I would love to hear yours. But I will not prod if you would rather not speak about it. Oh—I am Maya, by the way.'

Sujoy was surprised at the girl's empathetic tone. He wondered if anyone genuinely cared any more. His parents were long gone. They had lived in Kolkata all their lives, and after studying at Cambridge, Sujoy had moved to London, visiting India rarely. As for his extended family, he had never been the 'relatives type'. Cousins, aunts and uncles back in India had bored him even as a child. He had yearned for far-off shores. He remembered looking out of his room's window in Kolkata, beyond the street hawkers, the grime and the beggars, towards an unexplored horizon. The look in this girl's hazel eyes reminded him of that same longing. Strange how two strangers could share such a trait.

Since his fall from grace, Clara had pretty much stopped taking his calls. And they had been days away from moving in together. Chris, his supposed friend, had wasted no time in filling Clara in on the news and how Sujoy would lose his apartment in Park Street, Mayfair. Sujoy knew Chris had always envied him—his lifestyle, his ease with beautiful women. He now lived just outside town, in a far smaller place. Deep down, he wasn't even surprised by Clara's behaviour. He'd known all along that her affection was more for his lifestyle than for him. But he'd wanted nothing serious—not since *her* back in college.

'I believe every negative has a positive, and vice versa—the yin–yang,' Maya's voice broke his reverie. 'Your new job will give you the chance to meet people from different walks of life. London attracts people from everywhere; it is a melting pot of cultures. Who knows, you may just have a very interesting chance encounter.'

Sujoy looked at Maya through the rear-view mirror; the sparkle in his passenger's eyes made him feel hopeful. 'Maybe you're right. Better than making soap,' he joked. *You need to stop being out of line, Sujoy. This isn't a client's fancy office, and you are not the vice president of a bank anymore. Stop with the off-the-cuff remarks,* he reprimanded himself.

To his relief, Maya burst into laughter. *She gets my humour*, he thought. There was an earnestness in her voice, which made him feel cared for—something he hadn't felt in a long time. After his parents' deaths, he had felt more alone than ever. Work had kept him distracted, and he had ignored the fact that his 'friends' only used him for his connections and women were drawn to his affluence and wealth rather than him. He hadn't cared because a part of him enjoyed it—the power, the money, the respect in old boys' clubs.

He should have saved but, then, he had never envisioned a life without his job. He'd splurged on Birkin bags for girlfriends, vacations in St Tropez for hangers-on, and fancy cars for himself. Then, there was the gambling—a recent habit, but maybe that's what had made him take part in the fraud. Plus, he had no family to save for, after all. He sometimes wondered if he had not let go of his baby, would life have felt more meaningful and less lonesome, especially now when the going was tough? Where was the baby now?

Grown up, of course. The thought gave him goosebumps.

'Do you have any children?' Maya enquired.

Sujoy felt the hairs on the back of his neck rise. *Can this girl read my mind?* 'No, Madam. No family. Just me and...'

'And?'

'And the latest girlfriend who wanted a taste of my expensive life, but that seems to be a far cry now.'

'LOL.'

That's what my life has become—a big, fat 'LOL'. A 20-something girl, in my first week as a taxi driver has summed up my 47 years of existence.

As they turned around a corner, Sujoy spotted a sign up ahead, which read 'Heathrow Terminal 3'.

'We're here, Madam,' announced Sujoy, pulling to a stop and jumping out. 'Let me grab you a trolley.'

'This cannot be!' Maya suddenly shrieked, her hands rummaging feverishly through her Fendi bag. 'I have left my passport at the hotel.'

Before Sujoy could respond, Maya was already sprinting towards the Joy Airlines counter near the departure gates. Sujoy watched her flash a platinum card to an airport official, who quickly called over a young man in a purple Joy Airlines uniform. Moments later, she returned with him in tow.

'Sujoy, would it be possible for you to go back to the Four Seasons and fetch my passport? I left it at the reception desk while checking out. The airline is letting me wait inside and book myself on the next flight,' she explained, flashing her platinum 'Frequent Flier' card.

Sujoy nodded and set off, driving faster than he had in a long time. He felt an unexpected sense of purpose, a need to help this girl who seemed so genuinely worried. Her parents would likely be unhappy about her missing her flight, he thought. As he drove, he wondered how he would have been as a parent if he had kept his baby. A flood of sadness washed over him. So many things he wished he had done differently.

Maya knew her father would be irritated when he found out how careless she had been. He was the most patient and the kindest man she knew, but missing flights and not being on time were his pet peeves. He was her most favourite person in the world. She also couldn't stop thinking about her encounter with the ex-banker. He didn't seem like someone to be involved in fraud. Should she have asked him outright? Could she ask him later? Her iPhone started buzzing incessantly. She picked it up and smiled, 'Hi Dad! I was just thinking about you.'

Sujoy waited at the Four Seasons reception while the attractive blonde receptionist called Maya to double-check his credentials. He glanced around, taking in the luxurious interiors—the grand chandelier in the centre of the lobby, the royal red-toned leather furniture, the glitzy art on the wall and the hotel guests in their expensive clothes. Suddenly, it all seemed daunting.

'Here you are, sir,' the receptionist said, handing him a deep blue booklet. Sujoy tucked the passport into his inner jacket pocket and headed towards the exit. As he slid into his car, he paused, deciding to double-check the passport. Better make sure it's the right one; *I'd hate for her to be stranded*, he thought, recalling Maya's pale face at the airport.

He flipped the booklet open, reading the name on the first page—Maya Singh. His gaze dropped down to the lines: Father's name—Randeep Singh; Mother's name—Sheetal Singh. He had just pressed the accelerator, but upon reading the names, he quickly reached for the brakes. They let out a loud screech. *Could it be the same Singhs? It couldn't possibly be!*

The idea seemed impossible, insane even. With a pounding heart, he looked closer at the passport, finding an attached, older booklet inside. As he opened it, a younger Maya stared back, her hazel eyes gleaming. Then he found the undeniable evidence—a photograph tucked away within the leaflets.

It was a picture of an adolescent Maya with the very same Singhs he had met years ago. He stared at the photo long and hard. Randeep, smiling awkwardly, looked exactly as Sujoy remembered—his round face with the neat moustache, though now he had a slight paunch. And next to him, Sheetal's attractive face grinned back—a smile that started from her pink lips and reached her expressive kohl-lined eyes. Her jet-black hair was pulled back in a tight bun, a small silver bindi glistening on her forehead. She stood proudly by her husband's side in a floral sari. She looked just as she had on that fateful day, 25 years ago—the one and only time Sujoy had met them. Maya stood by the couple in a pink dress and white sneakers, her shoulder-length hair framing a face with a wide, toothy grin, as though she were posing for a toothpaste ad.

Is Maya my Muskaan? It sure does seem that way! It

has to be... Those eyes—just like her mother's. The revelation made him dizzy. He pinched himself; it felt surreal. Sujoy started the car and sped off, overtaking other drivers who honked furiously. It took him a couple of minutes to stop sweating and regain his composure. His hands trembled on the steering wheel, slick with sweat, and his vision blurred with tears. *Pull it together, Sujoy. You need to get to her on time. You need to show up for her at least once in your life.* Memories surged back.

It had been a freezing January morning in Cambridge. The loud, insistent banging on his apartment door pulled him out of a deep sleep. It was Rachel, his girlfriend of a year. They had met at a college party, and she was unlike any girl he had hung out with—kind, considerate and intelligent. She made him want to be a better person. Whenever Sujoy looked into Rachel's hazel eyes, his heart melted. On that day, however, as she stood outside his door, those eyes looked scared.

Rachel was pregnant and she wanted to keep the baby. Sujoy was stunned—they had always been so careful. Sure, he loved Rachel, but he had his future to think about, and his Ma and Baba back in Kolkata would never accept it. It was understood that they wanted a 'proper Bengali daughter-in-law' once Sujoy had settled into his job. An unplanned child with a foreign girlfriend? They would see it as nothing short of a scandal, blasphemous even.

Rachel had expected a proposal, but Sujoy hadn't proposed; their break-up wasn't easy on him. They graduated a month later, and Sujoy moved to London immediately, where he had secured an internship at Barney's Bank. In those early months, he missed Rachel immensely, but the long hours of work became his anaesthetic, numbing his feelings over time. A year later, however, came another loud knock on his door—this time at his tiny apartment near Tower Bridge. He opened the door to find Rachel cradling an infant in her arms.

She was there to leave their baby with him. She had found a man whom she wished to marry but that guy was unwilling to take in their child. Rachel was cold and unfeeling. Was this the same Rachel he had fallen in love with? It was then that Sujoy realized how people—whether good or bad—were often shaped by their circumstances at the time. He stopped trusting people and believing in strong attachments from that day forward.

For the first few days, Sujoy could think of nothing else but his daughter. She had pink cheeks and her mother's deep-set hazel eyes. Her soft gurgles and tiny cries stirred a new kind of love within him, one he hadn't felt before. He left the infant with a nanny for the first few days while he was at work, but soon it became impossible to afford one, and his work hours also became more and more intense. His parents were due to visit in a month, and he needed to think of some solution. After much deliberation, Rachel and Sujoy arrived at a mutual decision—a painful but inevitable one for Sujoy. They contacted an adoption agency, and, within a fortnight, they found a couple around their age, from India, Randeep and Sheetal Singh, who were looking to adopt.

Sujoy used to call his daughter 'Muskaan' in private, because of the way she smiled every time she saw him. It wasn't an easy separation. Sleepless nights haunted him for months afterwards. The experience left scars that no amount of time could heal; not a day had passed in all these years when he didn't think of her.

According to the arrangement with the Singhs, he was never to contact her unless she chose to seek him out.

'Who knows, you may just have a very interesting chance encounter sometime.' Maya's, his Muskaan's, words rang in his ears. He had imagined their reunion numerous times in his head, but never in his wildest dreams had he pictured such a strange tryst with destiny. *What would Maya think when I reveal that a potential crook she's read about in the papers is her real father?* The thought felt like a knife piercing through his heart. Sujoy drove like a maniac. So distracted was he by the voices in his head that he became deaf to his surroundings until a loud honk from a car behind shook him out of his trance. *Should I tell her? What should I do? What should I say?*

Sujoy couldn't keep pace with the zillion thoughts zipping through his brain. He wanted so desperately to see her again, look into her face and find which parts of her resembled him. He thought of the small gold locket he kept around his neck. Inside, nestled in two sockets, were pictures of him and Muskaan, taken just days before the adoption, and it was his only reminder of her. Sujoy had gotten an identical one made for her and given it to her adoptive parents. *Did they ever give it to her? Did she even know?* He had no way of knowing. He wondered if he should slip the locket inside her passport.

But if she didn't know, would it be fair to tell her like this? After all, hadn't he promised the Singhs that it would be their decision to tell her the truth.

He abruptly halted outside the airport departure gates and spotted the Joy Airlines employee standing exactly where he had left him. 'Madam has asked me to collect her passport from you. She wasn't feeling well and is resting inside.'

Sujoy felt the air evaporate from his lungs as a black cloud obscured his vision. For several minutes, he struggled to regain his bearings. Was this man going to take away his only chance to bid farewell to his child during their first bizarre encounter after so many years? Before he could gather himself, the employee snatched the passport from his hands.

'Please, at least let me speak with her when you get in. Give me your number so I know she has received the passport,' Sujoy pleaded. Suddenly, he realized he had Maya's number from the taxi app, and a spark of joy flickered within him, something he hadn't felt in years. The employee disappeared into the terminal. Several minutes later, Sujoy dialled a number, his phone nearly slipping from his clammy fingers.

'Hello Muskaa...I mean, Madam,' he stammered, his voice quivering. 'I hope you got your passport and have booked your flight?'

'Yes, I have. How can I thank you enough, Sujoy? I will be flying out later tonight. You know, you are going to be great at this job, I just know it!'

Sujoy's eyes welled up, and words also failed him. All that came out was a stutter before he heard a click. The line had been disconnected from the other end.

Maya flipped through the latest issue of *Vogue* in the airline lounge as she waited for her flight. Her phone buzzed with a message: *Dearest Maya, always keep smiling. The next time you are in your favourite city again, do give me the pleasure of showing you around. You were right about meeting good people along the way. And you are welcome to ask me my side of the story. I would be happy to share it with you any time. Sujoy Ghosh.*

Maya smiled, a wave of déjà vu washing over her. She saved the number, tugging on the gold locket she always wore around her neck. She did that out of habit, whenever she felt a pang of loneliness or emptiness. Her parents had given her this locket seven years ago, on her 18th birthday. Inside it was a picture of herself from when she had been a baby and an empty space for another photo. She had never quite understood why the other slot was empty, and whenever she asked her father, he would change the topic sheepishly. Maya couldn't wait to tell him all about her encounter with the banker cabby, Sujoy Ghosh.

When Life Gives You Lemons, Write a Novel

Life had played a cruel trick on Lily. Her husband of three years had walked out on her. While she was on the verge of a divorce, the countdown to the release of her first novel loomed—a novel that, among other things, spoke about an affair. A novel that was more non-fiction than fiction.

Lily looked around her rusty one-bedroom apartment that she had moved into with her blind dachshund, Rusty, after the confrontation with her husband. Rusty lay curled at her feet—the one thing that hadn't changed. The scene before her was a far cry, though, from the one she'd left behind: a four-bedroom house in the posh Golf Links locality of New Delhi, swapped now for a dingy flat in crowded Greater Kailash II with unfriendly neighbours.

But it wasn't the downgrade of the house or lifestyle change that irked her; it was the deep betrayal by a man she had thought truly loved her—a man she had fallen hopelessly in love with.

Lily had met Arun on the first day of the summer creative writing programme at City College, London. He was tall, dark and handsome—exactly her type. He had cracked witty one-liners (also Lily's type) whenever she was within earshot. He had noticed her in the expository class on the first day, where Lily sat alone on the last bench. Later, he confessed that his first thought on seeing her was, 'Why does such a beautiful woman look so timid?'

Lily had enrolled in the programme on a whim, worn down by years of waiting tables at a small but popular crêperie in St Christopher's Place. The day she first read *Harry Potter* had sparked her dream of becoming a writer, but now, nearly 30, she cursed herself for having let so many years pass without doing anything to make that dream a reality. The writing programme had been expensive by Lily's standards—£2,500 for seven weeks. But for Arun, it hadn't seemed costly at all. When they spoke after the expository class, he introduced himself with a firm handshake and a confident smile. She couldn't help but notice the gold Rolex on his wrist and the sweater with 'GUCCI' embossed in gold letters, paired with blue jeans. She remembered seeing the same sweater in the Harrods window display only days before.

His attire was too flashy for her taste, but once they started talking, Arun proved to be a surprising contrast to his ostentatious exterior. He had an easy-going, gentle demeanour. He worked in his family business, and writing, he disclosed, had always been a passion. Lily remembered how she had found the term 'family business' so vague, but when she eventually moved to Delhi a year later, she realized how common the phrase was.

Lily's parents were both professors at the London College of Economics, and they lived on the outskirts of London, in a small town called Pinner, where everyone knew their neighbours, and also the neighbours' neighbours. Lily, even at the young age of 10, couldn't wait to move to her city of dreams—London.

That finally happened when she turned 18 and enrolled in Economics at her parents' college. However, it wasn't long after she began her degree that she realized her true passion lay elsewhere. She didn't care much about the demand and supply of goods; it was stories that she found fascinating, and she yearned to create them.

By the time Lily was seven, she had read most of Roald Dahl's books, which were for children of 10 years and above; she had also read almost all the Enid Blyton titles available in the local library. By the time she was 14, Lily was asking the small town's librarian if there were more books by Gabriel García Márquez.

When Lily graduated in 2008, England was grappling with a recession. She had been slow to apply for jobs, and her 2.2 grade point average didn't favour her as a top candidate for research analyst positions in audit firms and investment banks. Even the second-tier, underpaid audit firms had no place for her.

An influx of foreign students—many of whom might have had 'family businesses' back home—were also competing for the same positions. 'After all, a stamp at Deloitte or KPMG for a year can only help our businesses,' she had once overheard a seemingly privileged Indian classmate remark in her development economics class.

Lily had no intention of returning to her small town, living with her parents and reacquainting herself with all her neighbours. So, she opted for the only other option available—waitressing at restaurants in London. Ten years passed in the blink of an eye, and she was lucky to find accommodation in Zone 2—Canada Water, to be precise—in the home of her cousin Susan.

Susan was twice removed from Lily's mother's side, and charged rent only every other month, at a heavily discounted price compared to the market. Lily speculated that this leniency stemmed from the fact that she was the only relative who had never participated in the 'Bully and Rag Susan' episodes during their childhood, when their entire family gathered for the holidays. In fact, Susan had actually fared better than all the other cousins who had bullied her in childhood and had the last laugh. She now worked as an investment banker, currently living in Hong Kong, and was posted to equally exotic destinations every two years. That certainly suggested that Susan was good at her job.

But such is fate: just when Susan was finally armed to face her bullies, family gatherings became rare. Relatives had either moved away in search of better opportunities, or passed away, or were just far too preoccupied with the humdrum of daily existence to meet up. They remained connected through the 'Royster Family' WhatsApp group, where Susan was noticeably quiet.

That particular afternoon, in her rusty GK apartment, with little Rusty still curled up at her feet, Lily suddenly felt a wave of nostalgia for London.

In her 12 carefree years there, in addition to waitressing, she had also spent two years working as a receptionist at a dermatology clinic—a job so boring that it made her go back to waitressing. She had few regrets; she saved a little from tips, caught up with friends on weekends and found the work easy. She also came across people from varied cultures and, for her, that was really the best part. She often imagined their stories, even though there was rarely time to put them on paper.

In the course of these waitressing years she had invented a game for herself. As she weaved between tables, whenever she heard a strange language, she would always try and guess what they were speaking. She recognized *Merci beaucoup, Je t'aime* and *Très bien* as French, *Namaste* as Indian, *Chia Chia* as Chinese and *Finito* as Spanish. And then there were dialects that puzzled her, and she would listen closely to the accents because that could give it away. Through the eyes, sounds and features of the people in front of her, she had vicariously visited these countries, wondering if she would ever actually, tangibly, be able to visit another country. That was the only time she regretted not having a better-paying job.

Then four years ago, something unexpected happened. Cousin Susan suddenly died. They said it was a car crash in Mumbai while she was on a four-day assignment there. The WhatsApp messages in the Royster Family group were sombre and to the point—hands-folded emojis accompanied by RIPs, with some relatives adding, 'Oh, how young! Poor Susan.'

So, ironically, the day Susan could have redeemed herself

in the eyes of her bullies never came and, instead, she was pitied, even in death, for dying too young.

A couple of days after the accident, Lily received an envelope—£10,000 in cash was enclosed within. It was some insurance scheme where Susan had named Lily as a nominee, entitling her to the proceeds. Lily wouldn't have bet £50 that she had meant that much to Susan. They only met a couple of times a year when Susan came home. But Lily did have a habit of underestimating what she meant to people.

After the unexpected windfall she enrolled into the creative writing programme that had teased her from the sidelines of her Facebook profile. Lily had spent years searching for writing programmes but always closed the browser, but now, the time had come to realize her dreams.

Snapping out of her reverie and coming back to the present, another thought clouded Lily's mind—how long would she have to live in this place? She had never lived alone in Delhi. Forget living alone, she had not even spent more than a few hours alone in the city. She stood up with some effort and reached for a dust cloth. Cardboard boxes full of her things lay stacked against the wall of the cramped living room. Through the creaky window, she could see a purplish haze covering the sky as dusk settled in.

Her phone rang, and a deep voice boomed on the other end: 'Hey, Lily! Deepak from Crosswords Book Shop here. Your reading is scheduled for 5 p.m. tomorrow. Don't be late, haan! It takes about 20 minutes from GK to Saket, but account for heavy traffic too. Use Google Maps but you can't always rely on those in Delhi.'

Click.

Lily felt a bit wobbly. This occasion—her book launch at a major bookstore in New Delhi—should have meant all and more for her under usual circumstances—if Arun was still around.

Back home in Pinner, her parents didn't have the faintest clue about her marriage falling apart.

Her dad had called her that morning when she was busy buying groceries.

'Hi Pumpkin.'

'Hi Dad, how are you? I miss you so much. Gotten rid of the sweaters yet?'

It was almost June, their favourite time of the year as a family.

'Yes darling, the sweaters are off, thank God. We are well, sweetie; how are you and Arun? We wish you were here to enjoy the summer with us. Oh, I know how you love home at this time! But we couldn't be more proud of you, honey. What a sweet day tomorrow—your book launch!'

Hi Dad, the next time I see you, there will be no Arun.

Instead she said, 'I know, Daddy. I couldn't have done it without you both—and Arun, of course!'

That was partly true. If Arun hadn't driven her to the edge of insecurity over the past year, there might have been no book.

It all began with Arun not picking up his phone at 6 p.m.—the time he usually left work and called her. An hour later, he would send a message: 'In a meeting. Will be home late.' And in a couple of months, he stopped showing up at home at all.

At first, when Arun simply came home late Lily gave him the benefit of the doubt. She knew a lot rested on his shoulders as the scion of Kapoor and Co., a fact he so often reminded all and sundry. Lily had never been the suspicious type. In fact, all her previous relationships had ended amicably, and she had been out with a variety of men—English, European... The most 'East' she had gone was Turkish, until Arun showed up.

When Lily married Arun, she quickly learnt that when you marry an Indian boy, you marry the family. Her mother-in-law, Mrs Kapoor, who lived just down the road, always told her every other day to come over for a cup of chai. But Lily knew that Mrs Kapoor would be busy with her kitty party friends, playing rummy; Lily also found the questions from her mother-in-law's friends intrusive: Why did Arun and Lily live by themselves? When were they going to have children? And on top of that, apparently Lily had to address them as 'aunty'.

Lily shared a cordial relationship with Arun's mother. Let's just say Mrs Kapoor never tread on Lily's toes, and going by the accounts of Arun's friends' wives—some of whom lived with their in-laws—this was the biggest blessing and flex in her marriage.

When Lily moved to Delhi she found that the physical transition was easier than expected. The city's old heritage, the colonial buildings, and the hustle and bustle reminded her of London, albeit Delhi was much filthier and disorganized.

It was the bored and bitter society that took more time for Lily to get used to. For instance, when they first moved to Delhi after getting married, Lily heard a little too many whispers about herself at the cocktail parties she and Arun frequented.

The circle Arun belonged to—considered 'upper crust'—could be vicious. Once, when she walked in hand in hand with Arun at his best friend's engagement party at the Taj Hotel, she heard someone say, 'The English gold-digger has arrived.' The comment was loud enough for both Arun and Lily to hear. It had been a mere few minutes after she'd draped a sari for the first time, excited to spend an evening with her new husband. Arun had confronted the woman who made that remark. Turned out, she had come into money herself only after the death of her second husband, who had been twice her age.

Lily did make some friends—Natasha and Anisha, both of whom had known Arun from school. Natasha was a successful fashion designer and Anisha ran a bakery from her home. Both were married and lived with their in-laws. They often reminded Lily how 'lucky' she was to have a sprawling mansion all to herself, without any 'interferences'. But Lily hadn't heard a bigger lie. Even though Arun's mother didn't live with them, she seemed to know everything that went on in their household—down to when she and Arun actually had sex, Lily was quite certain. This was thanks to the house staff who doubled as Mrs Kapoor's spies.

In the first year, Lily had no inkling of her mother-in-law's 007 nature. Mrs Kapoor was always so supportive, gentle and seemingly preoccupied with her own life. Lily enjoyed their afternoon coffee sessions, where she'd share her first-hand experiences of this strange yet exciting new land she had arrived in, on account of marrying her son. Little did Lily know that Mrs Kapoor was making mental notes of everything—how the party had been the night before, the people Lily spoke with, whom she liked or disliked, whom she considered her friends, and even what these friends were like, where they lived and how they dressed. Sure, Mrs Kapoor asked probing questions, but Lily dismissed them as just a mother-in-law showing interest in her new daughter-in-law's life.

Lily reached out for the cardboard box lying in the far corner of the room, next to the makeshift dining table. She picked up a bound stack of papers—the manuscript of her first book—and settled into the rickety armchair.

Chapter 1: The New Life

Tina had so much to get used to in this new life. It wasn't just the new country, or the bustling, chaotic new city where cows crossed roads at their whim and people danced all night in the streets without a care in the world, complete with a horse, chariot and blaring band. That was one part—the part where you felt like a cinema-goer, watching a marvellous theatrical movie. It was the part where she was IN the movie—the new Indian bride, the dutiful daughter-in-law and the revered memsahib being waited on—that was haunting.

A year ago, what now seemed like a previous life, it was Tina who waited on tables in London. Now, people waited on her in her sprawling new home. She knew many girls envied her position, her new dresses and the jewels she wore to the best social soirées in town. Yet, for her, it was never about the high life, but always the simple things that gave her so much joy.

Lily shut the manuscript and glanced around, looking for Rusty. He was lying under the table, his eyes wide open but blind as a bat. Tina's struggles were a reflection of Lily's own experiences as a newly wedded woman in a foreign land. Yes, Tina *was* Lily.

She remembered feeling lost, just like Tina, expected to act a certain way rather than how she wanted to. *This is how Meghan Markle feels*, Lily had thought. *But at least she's MEGHAN MARKLE. Everyone knows her. Who knows me? Do I make a difference to anybody?*

That's what had driven her to the animal shelter, where she'd found Rusty. The older dachshund, fragile and lost amongst the other big dogs, had a fierce bark, and Lily loved the way he had held his own. She adopted Rusty immediately and brought him home.

Arun didn't care much. As long as Rusty kept out of his walk-in wardrobe, which housed his designer shirts and shoes, he was fine. Occasionally, he would give Rusty a pat on his way out to work. Sometimes, Lily felt like she received the same kind of 'pat' and nothing more from Arun—none of the 'How was your day like, honey?'

It hadn't always been like this. The first six months were

heaven...for Lily and Tina both. Arun made the perfect lover and friend.

Lily began writing her book as an outlet for her emotions when she started suspecting Arun of cheating. Little did she know that she would end up writing less about the diverse foreigners she had observed so carefully during her time as a waitress in London, and more about the complexities of her own life.

Arun had been encouraging and had even laughed at the funny parts. Though he knew the general theme of the draft, he never suspected the story was about them. But then, Lily had only ever read the light-hearted sections aloud to her husband. It was Arun who introduced her to a publisher friend, who promised Lily he would read the first draft of the manuscript.

But yesterday, her dreams of publishing her book, like her marriage, almost came crashing down too.

There was a knock on her apartment door—it was Mrs Kapoor—still her mother-in-law, legally speaking. She had her usual bouffant, red lips, a baby pink chiffon sari pressed to perfection and her trademark black Chanel bag hanging from her arm.

'Lily! Oh God, Lily! What have you done?' exclaimed Mrs Kapoor.

'Mrs...Mom! Please come in!'

Even after three years of marriage, Lily struggled with calling another woman—not her mother—'Mom'.

Mrs Kapoor tiptoed inside as if she was entering a war zone, careful not to trip over imaginary bodies.

Sure, the apartment was tiny, dim and dilapidated, with

shabby furniture left behind by previous tenants. It was a far cry from the Kapoors' opulent mansion or even the home she had shared with Arun, where the chandeliers and floorboards were scrubbed to perfection every morning.

Mrs Kapoor was not one to be discreet. In fact, Lily was certain that the older Indian generation—like Arun's parents and their friends—probably didn't even know about concepts like being discreet or subtle.

For instance, so often she heard a loud belch or a fart after a hearty Indian meal from an elder Kapoor, and everyone let it pass as if it were routine. Initially, Lily had had to stifle her laugh, but had then grown accustomed to it. So much for being 'oh so proper'.

Perched on the sofa, Lily found herself smoothing out the fabric beneath her unconsciously. The woman in front of her had a strange effect on people; Lily had witnessed this first hand.

'Mom, please sit. Chai?' offered Lily.

Mrs Kapoor lowered her rather large bum on a corner of the sofa as though the rest of it would give her coronavirus.

'*Nahi nahi, kuch nahi.* You first tell me why in God's name have you moved here?' She gestured towards the room, waving her hands dismissively like an art critic appraising the shoddiest piece of work she'd ever seen.

Lily got up, paced and then sat down at the other end of the sofa, which let out a small groan. 'Mama, you know... about Arun—Arun and I—'

'Uff, I know everything! *And tu yahan chali aayi?*— And you moved here?' Mrs Kapoor kept waving her hands dramatically, like a thirsty bird searching for greener pastures.

'Things happen in marriages!' she continued. 'Okay, so he had an affair... So what? You're still his wife and our *bahu rani*, na! If you really wanted to move, he could have shifted you to our Chattarpur farmhouse or even the Defence Colony house. But what is this! This is how you insult us? By moving into a place like this? You know na, they'll talk about this at the Diwali parties...that the Kapoor bahu has moved into some shed fit for a *mali* (gardener).'

For a while, Lily blanked out. Her mind wandered back to Big Ben and the wonderful Hyde Park. She cursed herself for getting married into a strange culture and into a stranger family, and to a man who had betrayed her.

Had her mother-in-law really just turned the entire situation around on her! Never mind that her son had started an affair with a young heiress—someone fresh out of university, no less, and whose family owned an automobile company. That wasn't going to be the gossip at the Diwali parties. No, they'd talk about Lily, the bahu. Lily struggled to maintain her composure in front of this woman—her almost ex-husband's mother, who now resembled a large, angry bird. But despite her best efforts, she couldn't help the tears welling up in her eyes and making their way down her cheeks like a flooded river.

'Maa, I am sure you know that Arun was having an affair with Priya—Mr and Mrs Mehra's daughter. I mean, it's irrelevant who she is; what matters is that he was having an affair. And this isn't the first time. I feel so betrayed, Maa. I needed to move out and be on my own, not rely on Arun's means and yours... I mean, am I not Lily first? I know I am your daughter-in-law too, but as a person, Lily... my principles...'

Mrs Kapoor jumped to her feet. 'You *gori* girls! I had warned Arun! You only think of yourselves! What principles? *Hai hai, tauba*! "Am I not Lily first"! You were nothing before you joined our family! My Arun told me everything! Some waitress...'

Then she mumbled something under her breath, but Lily caught it, 'I toh had told Arun it's a mistake marrying a gori.'

Lily wasn't entirely shocked by these words. She had heard from her closest Indian girlfriends how, in their mother-in-laws' eyes, their husbands were akin to mini deities who could never do wrong. Arguments with husbands were best kept hidden, especially in households where everyone lived under one roof. But when the occasional explosive fight did happen and fireworks erupted, the after-effects were hard to miss—a dark cloud looming over the in-laws' moods, long after the couple had reconciled.

If these things happened, one could not tell at the huge social gatherings and opulent parties that were routine in this society. For instance, Natasha had a massive fight with her husband and felt her mother-in-law's wrath afterwards. However, at a Lohri party some hours later in a big socialite's home, where Natasha was dressed in a glittering red sari and matching red ruby set, Natasha's mother-in-law couldn't stop gushing about her. Such a farce it all was.

A first-person account of someone else invoked empathy but a first-hand encounter with the same experience stung deeper.

Sure, Lily had been a waitress, but she had also graduated from LSE. She had always been at the top of her class. She had advised Arun on his new glass bottle manufacturing business. Arun had once described Lily as an 'asset' to him, with her sound financial suggestions. He even said so at the family dinner table, which had earned her a small nod of approval and a hint of a smile from Mr Kapoor, a man who rarely smiled or showed emotion. And from Mrs Kapoor, a lady who was usually very expressive, it had only earned a grunt, a poker face and a tiny pat on Lily's back.

Lily snapped back to reality, knowing it was futile to reason with the lady in front of her. It's not like she blamed her completely; Lily knew Mrs Kapoor had been conditioned by a society where women stayed with their husbands, no matter what, and the birth of a male heir was considered to be the epitome of all accomplishments. Lily had heard stories of how Arun's birth—late in his parents' lives—had been met with a grand bash thrown by his grandparents because a grandson had arrived. Meanwhile, when Arun's *chacha* had a baby girl the following year, no such party was held.

Lily decided to remain quiet till Mrs Kapoor's tirade was over. She checked the phone on her lap; Arun hadn't called or messaged. It had been a week since she had moved out, and not a word from him. Suddenly, the realization struck—he had sent his mother to speak on his behalf.

Mrs Kapoor was tapping her heels impatiently against the floor, as if to get Lily's attention back. Lily looked up from her phone, her face now composed again.

Mrs Kapoor clearly wasn't done. Lily braced herself,

sensing that the real message from Arun was about to be delivered. Mrs Kapoor cleared her throat, a cunning look appearing across her face.

'See, Lily... Your book... Arun is quite disturbed by its contents.'

Now Lily was truly shocked. But she remained silent, letting Mrs Kapoor continue without saying a single word. She needed to hear this word for word.

'The reason why Arun hasn't messaged or called...' Mrs Kapoor paused.

Of course I know, thought Lily.

'...is that he feels you have been so engrossed in writing this book, where you have written an account of your relationship with him, about us and everything he has introduced you to... Maybe that's why the affair happened! Did you consider that? You have written about the affair too!'

Ever since she had started writing the book, Lily had begged Arun to read some chapters, but he was always tired. Once, she had read him a few pages, and he had loved them. As for a 'tell-all', it definitely wasn't. Sure she had woven the 'affair' into the story, but it resembled nothing close to what happened with them. It was Tina—her protagonist—who ended up having the affair and not the husband.

It was a twist Lily had introduced as a coping mechanism, a way of processing her own suspicions about her husband. Maybe it was a fantasy where she could redeem herself in her own stupid way. And now, this woman, standing in front of her—who hadn't read a word of her book—was accusing her of selling out the family, which honestly, wasn't even hers. The strangest part? Tina's in-laws didn't even feature prominently in the story as they lived in another city and seldom met.

Lily had always believed that, despite the complexities of Indian marriages, where one is married to the entire family, if there are chinks in the relationship, it still comes down to the two people at the core of it—husband and wife.

And this belief was the central theme of her first novel, *Tina's Story*.

The only element of truth she had borrowed from her real life was her experience of Delhi—its charm and chaos, and the society she 'belonged' to. But nothing else. In fact, Tina's husband wasn't like Arun at all.

And now, on the eve of her book's release, not only was her marriage crumbling, but she was also being accused of selling out a family she had truly loved. Should she protest? Maybe it was time she at least tried to put across her point of view. Confrontation had always been her weakness—she could pour her heart out on paper, but face-to-face discussions were a different story altogether. 'Mom, trust me. There is nothing about us—you, Papa, our family. It is a book of fiction and even there—'

'Our family?' Mrs Kapoor let out a guffaw, cutting Lily off. 'Beta, if this book comes out, there won't an "our family". *Vaise bhi* (Besides), Priya is a lovely girl. She may be a better fit...'

The way Mrs Kapoor said those last words—so matter-of-factly, in that plain tone—left Lily stunned. She had heard her mother-in-law use that same voice ever so often to tell the family *darzi* that the Manish Malhotra blouse was too loose and needed to be altered for a better fit.

A better fit? Was her mother-in-law telling her that her husband, who was having an affair, might have found a better fit in his mistress? And that a book of fiction was supposedly threatening Lily's place in the family she had called hers for three years?

Just as simply as Mrs Kapoor had walked in, she walked out, leaving Lily with, 'Think about it. You either choose that book launch you are having or this family and your husband. And don't bother calling Arun. He won't pick your call.'

Lily snoozed her alarm several times the next morning. Arun hadn't replied to any of her texts—explanatory messages about her book and pleas for him to read the parts that his mother had warned him about.

A part of her was furious that she was the one giving justifications when she had been cheated on. But then, love makes one do strange things.

At 9.30 a.m., when her phone rang for five minutes straight, Lily finally got up and answered it. It was Karan, her publisher and one of Arun's friends.

'Look Lily, please don't be late. The first book signing and reading is at 10 a.m. sharp. And since you are just around the corner, traffic isn't a worry, but we need to get out of there by 11 a.m. to make it to Saket by 11.45 a.m. for the next signing... I have a really good feeling about this! And get that husband of yours to miss his first meeting and come see his brilliant author wife in action. Bye!'

Karan had been encouraging Lily to write ever since

she had struck up a conversation about their mutual love for words at Natasha's Diwali cards party a year and a half ago. While Arun was engrossed in his winning streak at the rummy table, Karan was one of the few who had preferred to talk about anything other than cards. Lily had sent Karan a couple of short stories she had penned over the years and he had instantly liked one—a story about a girl navigating a new world. He had encouraged her to expand it into a full novel, and when she finally got down to it, Arun stopped coming home on time.

At first, Arun had seemed proud. He would listen with great interest when she read a snippet or two from the chapters. But later, he seemed preoccupied and indifferent. It all made sense to her now... He was obviously in 'affair mode' and not very interested in what his wife had to say. Lily had discussed the entire storyline with Arun, so when Mrs Kapoor accused her of writing something that had 'disturbed' her son, she couldn't in God's name understand what that even meant.

Maybe that was just an alibi. Maybe Arun wanted out and was now complaining to his mother like a spoilt six-year-old who isn't happy with his ice cream toppings.

As the dummy Big Ben clock on her new apartment wall struck 9.35 a.m., Lily made a firm decision, one she had been grappling with the entire night.

She showered quickly, dressed in a plain blue linen summer dress and wedge heels, and applied a touch of kohl to her brown eyes. She tied her blonde hair into a neat ponytail, added a pale pink lipstick and smiled at herself in the tiny bathroom mirror.

Carpe diem—she was going to seize the day. This was the moment she had longed for—a book reading of the novel into which she had poured in her heart, sweat and all the heavy emotions of the past year. This was not just her first novel; it was her first child, her newborn, and it needed her nurturing, even if it cost her her marriage. It was anyway a joke of a marriage to an immature husband.

Lily fed Rusty and took him down the stairs. She knocked on her landlord's door, and luckily, their 10-year-old son, Bunty, who liked Rusty, answered.

'Hi *Gori Didi,* you look so pretty. Hi Rusty!' Bunty beamed, flashing all his teeth.

'Bunty, I will be back by 6 p.m. Please don't leave Rusty alone. And I owe you a big treat for this.'

'Didi, don't worry. Even when I go to the bathroom, Rusty will come with me. I told you, I love him.'

Bunty proceeded to give a big hug to Lily, his pudgy stomach coming in the way, before taking Rusty's leash and disappearing behind the old wooden door.

Such a good kid, thought Lily, as she quickly booked an Uber.

Before she had walked out of Arun's house he had told her that she could always ask for the car and driver, and had even insisted that she stay at one of the other family homes—just as Mrs Kapoor had suggested. But it had been her decision to leave. He had told her that they could try to 'figure out their emotions' about what had happened by staying in the same house since it had four rooms, each far from the other. Why make a mockery of their family by moving out?

Family honour. Family reputation. Arun and his mother spoke the same language. But the double standards weren't lost on Lily. *Where was the family honour when Arun had an affair with a family friend's daughter, right under his wife's nose?*

Arguing with Arun would have been pointless. Lily had never been good at it anyway, and creating a scene wasn't her style. So, the day after her husband confessed to the affair, she packed her bags, found a place to rent online, checked out her landlord on Facebook and left in an Uber with Rusty. The house help had been napping, so her departure didn't raise any eyebrows. Lily had left as calmly as she had received the news of the affair. But the moment she got into the Uber, the flood of tears she had held back poured out.

The Uber pulled into the narrow lane outside her landlord's orange gate, Marked by a sign that read 'Guptas'—though the G could easily be mistaken for a C.

'Lily madam?' asked the driver.

'Yes,' she replied, still finding the 'madam' strange as ever, like something out of Victorian England. But she had long given up on correcting Indian Uber drivers by saying 'No, just Lily, please' because she knew they would just refer to her as 'madam' again.

'Marisons in Khan Market please, quickly!'

As she arrived at Khan Market, Lily jumped out of the car. Marisons was up ahead, and as she approached the bookstore, she noticed a book resting quite confidently among other titles in the glass window. It had a beautiful blue cover, with the silhouette of a blonde girl staring ahead at the cityscape that combined the Qutb Minar on one side and an urban market, such as the one she was standing in, bustling with people, stray dogs, beggars and cows on the other. The cover was a beautiful chaos, with 'New Girl in New Delhi by Lily Cooper Khanna' printed in a striking black font.

A surge of excitement and peace washed over Lily. Seeing her baby, her labour of love, displayed in one of Delhi's most famous bookstores could not be put into words.

What followed was equally surreal. The rest of the day Lily dashed from bookshop to bookshop in New Delhi, reading from HER book, signing copies, smiling for photos with eager readers, and moving on to the next event. Years later, she would look back and remember this day as one of the best of her life.

Many years later, Lily's books still graced bookstore windows, though now they were in far-flung cities—London, New York and even Istanbul. Shortly after her first book's release and the divorce that had left her broken, Lily decided to rise like a phoenix from the ashes.

She moved back to London, to her cousin's house, which apparently had also been left to her, though she hadn't cared about inheritance or money at the time. In London—the city where she felt most alive—she took a part-time job as a researcher in a marketing company and spent her free time writing. And once she began, there was no stopping her. Fifteen years after leaving Arun, his nosy family and New Delhi, something unexpected happened. Lily was at a quaint bookstore in Notting Hill, signing copies of her latest book. The line of readers snaked around the corner, and as she signed each book, a familiar cover caught her eye—the silhouette of a blonde surrounded by the chaos of New Delhi. It was her very first book.

Startled, she looked up. There, standing in front of her was Arun. He was older now, but still handsome—his thick black hair greying at the temples, his poised nose and high cheekbones lending him that same aristocratic air. But his eyes—his large eyes—held something different. Embarrassment, perhaps, as they met hers. They hadn't seen each other in fifteen years.

At first no one spoke, the seconds feeling like a lifetime. 'Hi Lily,' Arun finally said.

'Arun... I wasn't expecting you,' Lily managed to reply.

He smiled, but it was a shy, sombre smile—so different from what she remembered.

'I was in London for a conference and heard that a very famous writer was signing her new book in Notting Hill. I didn't want to lose the opportunity to meet her and get one of my favourite books of hers autographed.'

Lily smiled, feeling a shiver run through her as tears threatened to well up. Were they tears of joy, nostalgia or just that deep emotion one feels upon meeting someone who once meant everything to them after a very long time? Maybe it was all of it. Lily hadn't thought they would ever see each other again.

Arun gently opened the first page of the book and handed her a pen.

Lily, her hands trembling slightly, tried to shake herself

out of the reverie. She took the pen and wrote, the words flowing easily. 'To Arun, who I owe this book to, and the new me. If we hadn't met, the "new girl" in New Delhi would have forever been lost in every world.

Best, Lily'

She closed the book and handed it back, meeting his eyes warmly. They shared a knowing smile.

And then Lily turned back to the 100-odd people waiting for her autograph, winding their way through the charming cobbled paths of Notting Hill.

Serendipity, Lost and Found

Rajan thought it was her but couldn't be certain! She was just a few steps ahead on the busy street, her trademark long auburn hair bouncing loosely behind her. He quickened his pace, eager not to lose her around the bend.

And then he caught sight of that unmistakable face—sea-green eyes, a button nose and bow-shaped lips resting above a small but strong chin. The only thing that seemed different was the melancholy lurking behind the half-smile that had always been so characteristic of Janet. She held white carnations against her chest; those had been her favourite even back then. Her pale pink dress revealed that time hadn't altered her enviable figure.

After all these years, why now? Rajan thought, almost saying the words out loud. He recalled hearing through the grapevine that she had settled in London a few years back... so why was he so shocked? *Perhaps she is off to work.* He wondered if she ever started that publishing house she had always wanted to. As Rajan began to follow her, all thoughts of his urgent official meeting vanished into the cold London air, and he drifted into a deep reverie.

It was raining incessantly, very unusual for Delhi in

November. They were seated at their usual haunt—Cuppa Coffee—a delightful espresso bar nestled in the quaint market of Connaught Place. That place was special for many reasons; it was where they had had their first date, and many times later, they had often sat and chatted at that same corner table with a view of the outside world. Somehow, even the most mundane moments became exciting when shared with Janet.

She had a knack for cooking up stories on the fly; her favourite game was observing passers-by and imagining their lives. With her, even the roads choked with blaring traffic seemed to hold special meaning and exciting happenstance.

That November evening—he remembered it like it was yesterday—even the rain couldn't wash away the grief etched in the deep recesses of his being. He knew what was to come would change him forever.

'It is my excessively orthodox and volatile father,' she had tried to explain.

Her marriage had been 'arranged' to a 'Christian like her' ever since she was a little girl. Her mother was already suffering from a brain tumour, and Janet couldn't risk her health; the shock of marrying a Hindu boy would most definitely endanger her mother's life. She had resigned herself to her fate that they—Rajan and Janet—were not meant to be together. This meeting was her plea for him to accept the same.

'You have got to move on—and stay strong,' she had whispered, squeezing his hand.

He felt abandoned. Orphaned. 'But did you ever—' Before he could finish his question, Janet was already hailing a cab.

That memory was from six years ago. Rajan had never tried to stop her then, knowing it would be in vain. So why was he stalking her down the road now? He had a flight back to India in a few hours, and needed to head to his hotel and pack.

But he had always believed in serendipity. That's how they had met—Janet had been in the wrong theatre, seated in his spot. It was a funny story, and they had laughed about it for years afterwards.

He remembered her last words: 'You have got to move on.' Oh, how much he had tried to heed that advice!

'Beta, you do fancy women, na?' his mother had asked him over tea once. He almost reminded her that he had been in a relationship with a woman he adored for over four years. *Remember Janet, Mom?* he thought to himself but said nothing.

Rajan, now in his mid-30s and a successful investment banker, was an attractive and strapping man of 5 feet 11 inches. He had become the hottest topic of gossip among all the New Delhi aunties at their kitty parties. Everyone had tried setting up their daughters—and if they didn't have one, their nieces—with him. 'So sad... He's so eligible... Must definitely not be straight,' they murmured at social soirées, avoiding the word 'gay' as if they thought it to be an ailment that might be contagious to their own kin if mentioned.

Rajan followed Janet around the bend and up a staircase that led to a massive wrought-iron gate. *What is Janet doing at a cemetery?* The thought of being caught following her—and what he would say to her—flashed through his mind. Just then, she unbolted the gate and walked in; Rajan hesitated for a moment before slipping in after her, maintaining a safe distance.

She walked a few steps and then stopped in front of a white marble grave. Rajan, partially hidden behind a bush, was close enough to read the inscription on the tombstone.

'*Here lies Rupak Lee—Beloved Son, Brother and Husband. May he always Rest in Peace in the Heavens.*'

Rajan felt a sharp jolt in his chest, the same sensation he had experienced the last time he saw her—when she had hailed that cab. That name was much too familiar—*of course, it was her husband's!*

Janet laid the flowers on the grave and knelt down in prayer. Then she turned around and left through the gate as briskly as she had arrived.

Rajan stared into nothingness for a moment, feeling paralysed. A beep on his phone startled him back to reality. It was a message from Aisha.

'My dearest fiancé, I cannot believe we will be married in two days! Hurry back—I miss you. PS: Now those aunties will need a new topic for their luncheons since their favourite one—you—has been taken! Ha ha!'

Rajan replied almost immediately, 'I love you.'

Then he strode out from the cemetery and made his way down the lane opposite to the one his former lover had taken minutes before. As he walked down the cobbled street, his feet felt heavy in the expensive suede shoes he had bought the day before as a wedding gift for himself. They didn't look so new any more, soaked through by his unrelenting tears.

The Khanna Conundrum

How did he end up here—bankrupt, with his prized possession, his home, on the verge of being taken over? And that too by a bank that once seemed beneath him, almost insignificant, given his business and his family name; it wouldn't have even qualified as a contender to handle their accounts. He knew exactly how he'd gotten here, but that wasn't the point. The mismanagement and fund siphoning began when his trusted friend and adviser became the chief operating officer.

Varun, his numero uno since middle school, had recently returned to town after a seven-year stint in New York. He'd been fired by Lehman Brothers and was visibly depressed. But Varun was also brilliant and, above all, his best friend; he owed him. Varun had been there for him through thick and thin, from letting him cheat on those tough economics papers to lending him money when no one else would—not even his father—to start his business.

So, when Varun suggested a bit of creative accounting—a small diversion of funds here and there—it was hard to say no. After all, what harm did a little cheating do anyway? They had always gotten away with it as kids, hadn't they? Though he hesitated at first, it didn't take him long to get convinced, especially when he realized it meant that he could take his wife, the love of his life, Tara, on that second trip to the Maldives. It was a chance to reignite the romance; 15 years of marriage could always use a little spark, he'd thought.

Keeping the romance alive came at a price, and life was busy: his work, Tara's commitments to their son, tending to her ailing parents and, of course, hosting charitable soirées. These soirées, though ostensibly for good causes, were more about donning couture dresses and tasting the thrill of social one-upmanship with a glass of champagne in one hand. But now, he would have to break the news of their bankruptcy to her—the soirées would soon be a thing of the past.

The birth of the business idea—manufacturing 'brainy' toys for toddlers—coincided with the birth of their son, Virat. Tara had chosen Virat's name long before he was born; they'd always wanted one girl and one boy. The business concept seemed perfect; they had the machinery ready, repurposed from his father's now-defunct manufacturing business. His father had gone bankrupt 10 years ago, at least on paper. He always suspected that there was still some money stashed away somewhere. Late-night calls to overseas bankers in hushed tones from his father's home office had fuelled these suspicions. He'd overheard them during his own bouts of insomnia, which had set in after the bankruptcy hit them all.

The bankruptcy had forced a change in their lifestyle. His mother, the stiff-upper-lip socialite Mrs Khanna, could no longer indulge in her biannual trips to London or afford her weekly facials. She also couldn't keep updating the Khanna home's Italian marble every three years and changing the upholstery at will. But they could still host their classy annual Diwali party, which was enough to save face. Fortunately, the Khanna family home was theirs to keep, and he and Tara had a comfortable pad on the top floor. But he had always wanted to buy a house of his own, just to show his father that he, too, could make it.

It seemed, though, that such dreams were not meant to be. The impending bankruptcy wasn't terrifying—he'd squirrelled away enough money to keep them afloat for a while. Of course, the couture dresses would be a thing of the past, but one family holiday to a budget-friendly European destination could still be afforded. What truly terrified him was that his father, Mr Khanna, had no idea that he had put up the family home as collateral. Their beloved house, their jewel, was at risk—and so was their reputation. A legacy that his great-grandfather had built, his grandfather had elevated, and his father had preserved despite his own bankruptcy, was now on the brink of collapse. In this day and age, secrets like this were impossible to keep under wraps, especially as their bankers would love nothing more than to seize the house from him, relishing the fall of a family that once treated them with disdain.

The Khanna house was an imposing corner bungalow in the upscale Golf Links area of New Delhi. His great-grandfather had secured it—5,000 square feet of history—through a bold bid, before he even knew how he would pay for it. He had left everything behind in Lahore during Partition: their ancestral mansion, paint factory businesses, social circle and even club memberships. With his immediate family members, who had to leave one suitcase behind to make space for the family's two Labradors, he'd crossed over to India. They had huddled themselves into a bus with ripped seats, hoping for safe passage to a new country.

Although he hadn't met his great-grandfather, he had immense respect for how he had resettled the entire family in independent India, built another paint factory, then expanded into new businesses, and eventually bought the stately Khanna mansion where the family still lived. There was no talk of therapy or mental health back then; they just pressed forward. His great-grandfather lived to the plum age of 90, passing away from a sudden heart attack at a time when the business was at its peak. His grandfather stepped into his shoes and carried on the family's success.

Raj had always been in awe of that generation—how they endured hardships, without outlets like counselling. His father, though brilliant, was not a businessman. He had always wanted to get a PhD in Physics and study particulate matter. But Mr Khanna's father had other plans; so Mr Khanna completed his BSc in Mechanical Engineering and reluctantly joined the family business. Just as Mr Khanna was learning the ropes, his father passed away in his sleep.

And here Raj was now. He'd once promised himself he'd restore the Khanna name, re-establish the family business, and bring back its former glory. Yet everything had fallen apart. The toughest bit would be breaking the news to his father—who was so proud of the family home. Raj had always prided himself in the fact that he would at least be a better businessman than his father, but that didn't turn out to be true. His father hadn't gambled away their house. Raj should have never agreed to stake their home, for purposes of 'expanding' the business. Varun had nothing on the line except his reputation, which was not exactly spotless, but Raj had gambled everything.

Raj chose a few days before his father's 85th birthday to break the news; it couldn't wait any longer. The bank had already intimated that they would seize the house in the coming week.

At around 8 p.m., Mr Khanna was in the family den, as he was every evening, sipping his one weekly glass of beer. The BBC news usually droned on in the background, but that night, as Raj entered the den, he noticed his father going through an old photo album. This was not going to be easy, and Raj, an otherwise confident, articulate man, was often tongue-tied in his father's presence. It was a dilemma that had presented itself to him when he was 12, and at 55, it had not become any easier. Raj cleared his throat, feeling his voice tighten.

'Good evening, beta,' Mr Khanna greeted him in his crisp British accent, a remnant of his days of studying in England. Even at that moment Raj could picture his father as a professor at Imperial College, where he had pursued his bachelor's in Physics, before being called back to handle the family business.

How different life might have been for him, Raj thought with an ache, now looking at his father's almost all-white hair, which was neatly combed to one side. *This man is really better than you,* Raj told himself, fully conscious of his own receding hairline. *He has managed to keep a full head of hair and a house for his family. You couldn't do either.*

As if he could sense something off, Mr Khanna asked, 'All okay, puttar? Tough day at the office? Come, sit with me and have a beer.' He patted the space next to him and added, 'I want to show you these photos—of your great-grandfather and his brothers before the Partition. They would have been so proud of you, seeing how you turned the business around.'

Raj swallowed hard, fighting back tears. For the next half an hour he sat silently, gazing at the black-and-white photos of his ancestors, their dignified faces staring back at him. But instead of pride, he imagined disapproval in their eyes, as though they could see right through him, nodding their disdain.

As Raj flipped through the sepia-tinted memories of his lineage, his heart tightened with guilt and dread; each photograph seemed to echo his failure louder than the last. He wanted to confess, to unburden himself of the weight of deception. But the fear of disappointing his father, of shattering the last semblance of pride Mr Khanna held in the family name, kept him silent.

With each passing moment Raj felt the shadows of regret creeping over him. He glanced at his father, his hero despite their differences, and a lump formed in his throat. How could he tell this man, who had sacrificed his dreams for the family's legacy, that he had jeopardized everything?

Raj's phone buzzed incessantly, multiple missed calls and messages flooding the screen, from Varun and the bank. He felt his stomach churn. The Khanna house was non-negotiable; it would be gone.

'Excuse me, Papa,' he said meekly, slipping out of the den.

Over the next few days, paranoia gripped Raj. He constantly checked the news online, scanning for any exposé, leaked documents or accusations plastered across with the headline: 'Businessman Raj Khanna Under Investigation for Financial Fraud'. The fear that his secret was moments from exposure gnawed at him, and he felt his carefully crafted life on the verge of unravelling. Soon everyone would know. His wife and son, whom he adored, his mother, who would certainly be the least forgiving, and his father, who he wanted to protect more than ever.

As his father's birthday dawned closer, Raj made a decision. After the party, he would sit the entire family down and prepare them for the storm. They would move to a temporary rented accommodation until he could negotiate a solution with the bank.

Yet Raj couldn't have foreseen the way the evening would unfold even in his worst nightmare. Even all these months later, Raj wished that the earth had split open so that he could have dived in before all this happened. The evening of Mr Khanna's 85th birthday arrived, the house pulsing with the energy of New Delhi's jet set, as they streamed in through the golden gates of the Khanna mansion. Guests mingled, laughter echoed, flutes clinked, and the air was thick with the aroma of delicacies—from caviar to Italian truffle.

But amid the gilded spectacle, Raj felt a burning tension building inside him. Standing by the floor-to-ceiling windows, he glanced outside and noticed the sky that seemed to be preparing for a massive storm.

Raj gulped down his Dom Pérignon and heaved a sigh of relief. Maybe no one would come after them and things would get resolved. He would ask for a bit more time from the bank; hadn't they ridden the wave of success with him when he had entrusted them with a small account to manage? He decided to enjoy the party. It was time to mingle with the guests and take care of them.

Looking around, Raj saw Tara shimmering in a silver sari and his mother exuding elegance in a gold brocade one. He knew about saris because as a young boy, he had often spent time in his mother's walk-in wardrobe with her.

Virat, his son, grinned from across the room, and Tara gestured for him to join her. An old friend of his father's, Malhotra Uncle, struck up a conversation with him about the good old days. Just as the champagne's light buzz began to ease his mind, he felt a tap on his shoulder. It was Chotu, their house help of three decades, who despite nearing 50, could pass for a 35-year-old. '*Chote saab, aap study mein aayenge? Bade saab bula rahein hain.* (Sir, will you come to the study? Your father is asking for you.)'

Raj felt a pit form in his stomach. Excusing himself from Malhotra Uncle, he made his way to his father's study. The guilt weighed heavily on him, making it hard to walk in his Italian shoes. He wondered how his father would feel when he would have to pack up his prized possessions from the den. As he neared the den, his heart raced; he had just been intimated by Varun that the banker would be arriving sooner rather than later.

Mr Khanna seemed lost in the past as he sat flipping through the pages of old albums. He seemed oblivious to anything untoward, even the festivities taking place outside, a peaceful look on his face. Raj wanted to take a picture of his father looking tranquil, fearing it might be the last time he saw him like that. He entered hesitantly, hoping to his father alone before the inevitable confrontation.

'Beta,' Mr Khanna began warmly, 'the party is going very well. But after it is over, I would like you to glance over my will. There are some things you may be unaware of.'

Before Raj could respond, a sharp knock echoed through the room. He knew this signalled the arrival of the banker. Without waiting for permission, a middle-aged man in a suit entered, his professional façade barely concealing the urgency of his task.

'Mr Khanna, I apologize for the intrusion, but urgent matters require immediate attention,' the banker stated, looking at Raj with an inscrutable expression.

Mr Khanna, his brow furrowing slightly, motioned for the banker to continue. Raj felt his stomach churn, knowing the moment of reckoning had arrived far sooner than he had anticipated.

'Mr Raj Khanna,' the banker's voice was firm, laden with authority. 'I regret to inform you that the bank has initiated proceedings to claim this property due to outstanding debts.'

Raj's heart skipped a beat, the words landing like a physical blow. He cast a desperate glance at his father, hoping for a miraculous intervention or a reassuring gesture, but Mr Khanna remained silent, his expression a mix of concern and disappointment.

The banker outlined the bank's plans, citing legal obligations and timelines as the birthday celebration buzzed faintly in the background—a stark contrast to the grim reality within the study.

Raj felt a wave of despair wash over him, and he struggled to find words. His secret had been exposed in the most humiliating manner possible and at the worst possible moment—right in front of his father, during a celebration meant to honour him. He had even prepared a speech—a thank you to his father, to highlight the man of substance that he was.

Though visibly distressed, Mr Khanna held his composure. He exchanged a brief glance with Raj—a look that carried both regret and a plea for explanation.

As the banker concluded the revelation, Raj stood there, a maelstrom of emotions swirling within him. The '70s Bollywood songs from the other room seemed like a distant melody, a cruel contrast to the turmoil within the walls of his father's study. The confrontation had unfolded, and the stark reality of their impending loss now hung heavy in the air, casting a pall over the once tranquil environment.

As the weight of the banker's revelation settled over the study, Mr Khanna reached into the desk drawer, pulled out a set of papers, and held them out to Raj. 'These were in the will,' he said in a measured tone.

Raj took the papers, scanning the lines that detailed substantial investments in science-backed stocks that Mr Khanna had safeguarded for dire situations like this.

Even when his business had crumbled, Mr Khanna had managed to invest their remaining wealth in profitable avenues. The irony struck Raj hard; he had always seen himself as the family's 'saviour', while his father, whom he'd viewed as a 'failure', had actually held the real safety net all along.

Frozen in place, Raj felt a rush of shame and regret rise in his throat. Just then, Mr Khanna's phone buzzed. His fingers trembled slightly as he checked the message and a look of relief washed over his face—a glimmer of hope in the face of imminent adversity.

With calm authority, Mr Khanna addressed the banker, 'I appreciate your diligence in this matter. Rest assured, we will settle our obligations as per the agreed terms.'

The banker, slightly taken aback, quickly resumed his professional composure. 'Yes, sir. We look forward to hearing from you. Oh, and a very happy birthday.' With that, he left the study.

Raj, visibly shaken, turned to his father, ready to face the repercussions of his actions. Tears streamed down his face and he could not utter a single word. Neither spoke for what seemed like an eternity. The silence was finally broken by the creak of the door. Tara and Mrs Khanna stood frozen in the doorway, their faces a portrait of dismay. It was clear they had overheard the unsettling conversation.

Tara's eyes, filled with tears, met Raj's, reflecting the hurt and disbelief she felt. Mrs Khanna's features were carved with a mixture of anger and despair as she surveyed the scene with a piercing gaze.

'What have you done, Raj?' Tara's voice quivered, thick with anguish and betrayal. 'How could you do this to all of us?'

Raj, still struggling to find words, turned to his father for support, but Mr Khanna's gaze remained fixed on the floor, his face stoic. He stepped forward, revealing his father's secret investments, explaining how Mr Khanna had safeguarded them for moments of crisis like this. But it did little to ease the searing disappointment etched on Tara's and Mrs Khanna's faces.

An icy tension pervaded the room as Raj stood there, haunted by the consequences of his choices, torn between gratitude for his father's unexpected support and the overwhelming guilt as he felt his family's unforgiving gazes pierce through him. Within the study, an unspoken rift had torn apart the fabric of trust and love that once bound them together.

Mr Khanna finally broke the silence. He motioned gently for them to come together. 'This is when we stay together,' he said quietly. It was clear—despite the storm of emotions, as head of the family, he had an unwavering determination to salvage what he could. With a composed demeanour, he gestured for Raj, Tara and Mrs Khanna to accompany him back to the party.

For a moment, the family stood hesitantly at the threshold of the ornate living room, caught between the whirlwind of emotions and unresolved conflicts. Then, almost in unison, they stepped forward, re-entering the birthday celebration as if nothing had transpired in the study.

Tara, regaining her composure, motioned to Virat to come forward. 'It's time to cut the cake!' she announced, guiding him towards the cake table where his grandfather was waiting.

Amid the laughter and chatter, the family donned masks of composure, concealing the strain beneath forced smiles and polite exchanges. Beneath the polished façade, however, lay the unresolved turmoil that had unfolded in the study.

Mr Khanna maintained an air of dignified grace, steering conversations and ensuring the festivities carried on seamlessly. His unwavering composure served as an anchor, a silent plea to his family to set aside their grievances—at least for the moment. Raj, Tara and Mrs Khanna attempted to follow suit, engaging in polite conversations, exchanging strained pleasantries and participating in the celebrations with a resolve to preserve a semblance of unity. It was a fragile peace, a delicate truce, held together by their shared commitment to the family name and the evening's celebration. After the cake was cut, Mr Khanna turned to Raj and said, 'I guess your friend Varun didn't have the guts to show up.'

Raj was stunned. His father knew. Mr Khanna had always warned Raj about Varun, never approving of his best friend, who was almost like a brother, and it had been a point of tension between them since Raj's youth. As tears welled up in his eyes, Raj looked down at his blue Berlutis. He wanted to take off the shoes and hit himself with them. He felt unworthy of the fine shoes he wore and unworthy, too, of inheriting the responsibilities of the family's legacy. He knew it would be a long road to forgiveness from his mother and even Tara.

As the celebration continued, the family members moved through the evening, their hearts heavy with unresolved conflicts and unspoken apologies. They held on to the facade of unity, their unspoken grievances overshadowed by the necessity of presenting a united front.

And as the night wore on, a quiet realization emerged among the Khannas. They could no longer rely on appearances and polite exchanges to hold them together. To truly mend the fractures in their family, they would need more than forced smiles and celebratory toasts. They would need heartfelt conversations, forgiveness, and a collective willingness to mend the fractures that threatened to tear them apart.

For now, though, the Khanna name and the mansion that bore it had been saved. And for the time being, that was enough.

The Life of Three

January 2015

'Hipooooo, my darrrrling Hipooo! This term was just tooooo much of fun,' Samara drawled in an accent that sounded quite strange to him. Harpreet Singh, affectionately known as Hippo, was an affable Sardarji from Chandigarh, a beautiful town in north India. Everything about Hippo was average, except for his facial features. He considered his looks below average: a small but rather hooked nose reminiscent of a baby eagle's, beady eyes and, to top it, the mandatory beard that was getting unruly by the day. He even swore a bird almost made a nest in it the last time he fell asleep on the terrace.

Samara, originally from Ludhiana, spent a lot of time in Chandigarh, as her parents shuttled between the two cities, partly for work and partly for social commitments. Coming from an affluent Punjabi family, she was the only child, the apple of her parents' eyes, social and attractive to the point that she had more than a few 'friends' falling for her now and then. What Hippo found most baffling about his best friend was that she remained mostly oblivious to these sudden romantic interests she sparked in many hearts—including his own.

'I am shhhhure it was, yaar! I mean, when can Lundun not be fun?' replied Hippo in his Punjabi accent, unlike Samara's acquired English twang. 'I know I have not been, but from all your talks—first from your summer holidays and now since you have started studying there—'

'Oh Hippo! Do you know that I actually landed tickets to the London Fashion week?' Samara cut in, not paying much attention to what Hippo had been saying. 'I mean, all thanks to Daddy, of course. He just called up that Hampstead-wale Mehra uncle and got me two tickets, that also last minute. I took Lucie—you know, the French girl I mentioned?'

Samara had returned from London with all the airs of a modern aristocrat, though she secretly cherished and only related to her desi side. Nobody knew this better than Hippo. Recently, he had also realized that he was hopelessly in love with her. What he couldn't figure out, though, was what was worse—that she had no inkling about his feelings or that he always had to hear about her latest fling, swallowing his pride and tears, and pretending to be happy for her. It had been a year of this, ever since Samara transferred to Brooksmead School in London. Hippo couldn't help but feel a bit jealous—mostly about the other boys, but sometimes about her carefree ways, too.

There were many things about Samara that had made Hippo like her—her opinion about everything under the sun being one of them. Samara always had something to say about everything, whether it was the present government, the latest fashion trends or the newest restaurant in town. It was always interesting to be around her.

But what Hippo loved most about Samara were the

insecurities she secretly nursed. He found that these made her more attractive and only he, along with a select few, had an 'in' into this secret garden of vulnerabilities. In a world full of people disillusioned by their own overestimated intelligence, this trait of hers was appealing to Hippo. To the world, she was the young, confident Samara, but the sheer vulnerability that she shrouded under layers and layers of opinion and verbosity was something he had sensed all along.

The timing of his romantic feelings, however, couldn't have been worse for Hippo. His 12th-grade board exams were around the corner, and he needed to ace them, get into a decent college and fulfil his father's dreams. After all, Hippo wasn't born with privileges and a silver spoon in his mouth. His father, Mr Singh, had worked very hard as an accountant in a private firm for 30 years to provide their family with a decent standard of living.

He found stark differences between his best friend's upbringing and his own. While Samara was the heiress to a thriving textile business, which her grandfather had founded, Hippo had always lived on a budget. His pocket money never exceeded a certain measly amount and his good friends often treated Hippo in the canteen. Samara, on the other hand, had never not spent a summer holiday in a foreign country. Summer holidays for Hippo meant his Nani's house in Shimla, the highlight of the trip being a kulfi at the mall. If he were to compare it to a Bollywood movie, his holidays would be like *Piku*, While Samara's resembled *Dil Dhadakne Do.*

There was also no doubt in Hippo's mind that soon after college Samara's father would begin introducing her to 'suitable boys'. By then, she would likely have tired herself out with her 'fly-by-night' and 'just a pastime' pursuits. Already, her internships changed more frequently than her designer wardrobe—one month she was working at a zoo; the next she wanted to be a chef.

'I am telling you, Hippo, I am very serious this time. Fashion design is my calling!' Samara had declared. 'You see, after two years at the London School of Fashion, I will launch a collection—fusion clothes, an 'East meets West' line; it's going to be inspired by my travels around the globe.'

Hippo had heard stories about his father's struggles right from childhood. Mr Singh was the son of an English teacher in a small government school in a Punjab village called Hoshiarpur. Mr Singh's father had put all his meagre earnings into educating his son in a decent school, located in a little town some 20 km away. Mr Singh would wake up at 5 a.m. every day to hitch a ride with an uncle who worked in the same town. Though the school began at 7.30 a.m. Mr Singh reached an hour early to brush up on the previous day's lessons. He went on to become an accountant and worked in a reputed company all his life. He was able to provide his family with a far more comfortable life than his own childhood—when some days he'd go to bed hungry.

Hippo was well aware of their humble past and this weighed on him heavier than anything else. Having been a fairly average student throughout his school life, he often felt that he had disappointed his father. Being distracted with thoughts of a broken heart wasn't going to help.

September 2016

Israel was turning out to be a fun trip. In just a few weeks, Samara and Yunus, her new Israeli 'friend', had formed a close bond Samara had met him only days after landing in Tel Aviv, while touring the Beit Hatfutsot—The Museum of the Jewish People, located inside the Tel Aviv University campus. Yunus, who worked as a tour guide there, had caught her eye near the ticket counter. Tall and lean with dark brown, side-swept hair and a wheatish complexion, he was distractingly handsome, with bushy 'caterpillar' eyebrows above glinting eyes and peach-coloured pouty lips.

'You are at the wrong counter, Miss—women to the right,' Yunus said shyly, in an accent that was foreign to her ears. He had briefly glanced at Samara but looked away almost the next second, as though making eye contact while speaking might be deemed inappropriate. She couldn't help but notice his dimpled grin and his long eyelashes.

'Oh, I did not notice that sign—but now that I do, how right it is! And the pun has been used well,' Samara replied, laughing at her own witty one-liner. Yunus smiled back, though his confused look suggested he probably didn't understand what 'pun' meant.

How cute he looks even when he's awkward, she thought.

'Yes, people mostly never notice that sign, but women

are always right,' Yunus replied, this time looking straight into Samara's eyes, almost as if reading her mind. 'Would you like a tour guide?'

'That would be great!' Samara blurted out without thinking, her heart fluttering. *I hope he doesn't notice my flushed cheeks—or hear my heartbeat*, she thought.

Convincing her father to let her visit Israel, however, had been another story. 'Daddy, I want to go to Israel over the short October break. You know I have been reading about the culture anddddd—'

'Not over my dead body,' her father had sternly interjected, pretty much ending the conversation. Mr Khanna had his reasons. The Israel–Palestine conflict had heightened over the past few days; all the news channels only seemed to be reporting stories of bloodshed on both ends. He knew it would not be safe to travel to the country, though he visited the country on various textile export delegations but during better times.

The thought of visiting Israel had hounded Samara even more after her father's no-nonsense 'NO'. She devised a simple plan: she would tell her parents she was going to visit Ann in Cardiff for her break, but then head to her dream destination, Israel, instead. They would buy her story and even encourage her to roam and explore the English countryside.

Why hadn't she told Hippo about the plan? They had drifted apart. Her best friend from school had now become a different person. He had managed to get into a good university to study law—Punjab University in Chandigarh. Samara couldn't bear to hear another lecture on corporate tax or torts. Also, Hippo no longer seemed to have time for her. Even during holidays, when she had visited home and asked Hippo to go out for lunch or a movie, he was too busy with his study dates at a college friend's house. And his college friends were another story.

The day Samara met Meera was an unusual one. Firstly, it never poured that heavily in July in Beersheba in southern Israel. That day, it felt as though the skies were finally letting out days of pent-up emotion. Samara and Yunus—now her boyfriend—had just finished touring Tel Aviv and Haifa. Yunus had insisted they come down to the south. 'No, it's not all coastal and Mediterranean,' he had stated. 'You must see entire Israel.'

Yunus himself was from Tel Aviv, and had felt a need to explain the different demographics of the country, probably forgetting what a diverse country Samara herself came from. But she didn't say this out loud; she was in love and didn't want to hurt his feelings—very unusual for Samara as she had always voiced what she felt with her previous crushes. She didn't quite understand why this one was so different.

As they walked past the engineering university, they came across a tall girl with long brown hair and a frail frame, who was struggling to open her umbrella, caught in an impromptu Marilyn Monroe moment as her skirt blew up in the wind. Even from a distance, Samara could tell that the girl was strikingly attractive. She could also sense that she was playing the role of a 'damsel in distress'.

'Hi! Do you need help?' chirped Samara.

What started as a friendly remark to a stranger soon blossomed into a friendship between two girls who may have had nothing in common except for being alone in a foreign land. Their association ended up going a long way, longer than either of them could have ever imagined.

January 2025

She had followed the same routine every single day for the past 10 years now. Every evening at five, she would return to her writing desk. After penning a few lines in her diary, she would drift into a deep reverie—about a world that now seemed like it belonged to another lifetime. She would then look at her face in the broken mirror on her desk, noting the strands of grey outlining her forehead and her unkempt hair spilling on to her lap. Even after all the years of hardship, she was surprised to see a twinkle in her eyes.

Today, she had resigned herself to her fate—locked up forever, with no one to care about her. As she peered out of the decrepit window, the only one in the poorly lit room, she noticed the overcast sky. She took up the yellow piece of parchment in front of her and wrote:

The Sky Today

The sky today is the face of a man
Bursting with a multitude of feelings,

> Holding back tears,
> Trying to conceal the pain;
> But scars of unrealized dreams
> And dashed expectations burst at the seams.
> The sky today is so full of emotion,
> Like a man who smiles from ear to ear—
> Big, 'cloud-filled' grins,
> Loneliness disguised under unsatisfactory wins.

How did this all begin? Such weather often made it worse than most days. Even though a long decade had passed, she still got flashes of a life long gone—a completely different life, full of happiness, love and luxury, thousands of miles away.

She peered down at her notes—pages and pages of poetry, all with the same theme: longing. She tore an empty sheet from her long notebook and started writing again. This time, she addressed a living being. 'Dear, if you ever read these... I used to count the days, but now I only know it's been 120+ months... It's strange when it's been that long and you are hearing from a person you once knew. It definitely feels like a different lifetime or as if that person never truly existed. Well, you existed for me... You still do, in my memories... I wonder if you have kept me alive in yours.'

Her signature smudged as tears fell on to the page. Before she could re-scribble her name—her real name, her birth name, the name that once held her identity—a knock at the door interrupted her.

She blamed herself for her fate every single day, going back to that same overcast day in July, when the sky poured out days of emotion. Why did she ever befriend her?

Why didn't she leave as scheduled?

The knock on the door had been Nusra, her house help, bringing her evening tea and biscuits. 'Madam, within one hour, you must take your medicine,' she reminded her in a gentle tone. Nusra was probably the only one who slightly cared. Or maybe Nusra just felt bad for her.

She nodded an affirmative and attempted a weak smile.

The medicines always made her groggy, but over time, she had come to like them as they also made her reveries more real. She swallowed the two orange pills. It was only a matter of minutes before they started to take effect. She reached for the white cup on a floral tray by her bed lamp, her hands trembling. The contents inside swirled—a brown whirlpool like a river, rich in soil, doing an orchestrated dance. She noticed the golden rim and the figurines wearing lace gowns adorning the white teacup. She imagined this was what women wore during the 1920s in England, such as in her favourite book, *Little Women*. Her grandmother had gifted the book on her 15th birthday. Tea always reminded her of Grandma.

The low whistle of the kettle in the kitchen while they sat in the dining room—Grandma and her; she was at Grandma's place in the countryside for the weekend. It was one of those visits, days before her 15th birthday, where she would finally hear about Grandma's captivating past. It was that story that would seal her fate.

All these years, she had blamed herself for her destiny, but now, for a fleeting moment, she wondered—*could Grandma share some of the blame? No*, she concluded. *Fate itself was to blame.*

The medicines had taken effect. Alternating between moments of dream and lucidity, she managed to reach her bedside drawer and pull out a plastic packet of purple powder. She had found it during her fortnightly visit to the supermarket, one of her rare outings—supervised, of course. She couldn't remember the last time she had managed to go out of the premises unsupervised. She emptied the packet into her tea. *Hope it tastes good*, she thought. Her afternoon tea was one of her only pleasures of the day. Since this one was going to be her last, she didn't want it to be any different—–because on that overcast day, she, Aaliya Begum, had decided to end her life.

October 2025

As he stood at the far end of the courtroom, seconds before the final verdict, Hippo Singh already knew what was coming. The judge ordered the courtroom to be silent with a loud thud of his hammer. It was in the next few seconds that Hippo felt his world fall silent, as if he'd gone partially deaf. He drifted into a state of hypnosis, lost in visions of his early days with his now-deceased wife, Natalya.

Hippo met Natalya in his final year of law school. She had come to Punjab University as a foreign exchange student from Pakistan, and she was that girl everyone noticed. Her long brown hair, emerald eyes and alluring smile made some weak in the knees and others cautious. Her gaze held a distant look, a suggestion that they had seen much grief. But nothing else in her demeanour hinted at that; she was always warm and seemed to have grown up being used to getting affection.

When Natalya joined college, others had long found their cliques, since it was the final year. No one had time for niceties and the atmosphere was getting more competitive as the year was ending. All anyone cared about was who would get that coveted apprenticeship with the top criminal lawyer or in Malhotra & Malhotra, the top law firm of the city. Things were getting tense for these young adults, and Hippo was no exception. He had his own father to prove himself to.

At first, Hippo ignored Natalya's advances. She would text him at odd hours, but he couldn't understand why she—an attractive girl, way out of his league—would be interested in an average Sardar like him, especially when the high-cheekboned Karan had shown interest in her. *Does she need help with college work?* had been Hippo's initial thoughts. Later, things took a different turn. Romance blossomed between the two or something like that. Natalya had been persistent, and his parents liked her.

'Why not settle down? Ask for her hand or she'll ditch you soon!' his mother often nagged at the dinner table.

'Haan, your mother is right,' his father agreed one day, tired of his wife's nagging.

Natalya and Hippo had wed exactly five years ago in a small Punjabi ceremony in Chandigarh. A handful of their mutual friends from college attended, Karan included. Hippo's school friends weren't present; after all, his one and only close friend from school, Samara, had long vanished from his life—from all their lives. Her parents also didn't attend.

Saying that the shock of Samara going missing had been too much for the Khannas would be a gross understatement. Life as they knew it had ceased to exist. It happened 10 years ago, and every day after that, Mr Khanna used all his connections to try and find his beloved and only child. After multiple trips to their daughter's last-known whereabouts, visiting friends and acquaintances from around the world, and launching an international investigation, there was still no trace of Samara. The Khannas eventually migrated to Vancouver, Canada, never to return, donating their house to a Christian missionary school.

Were they still looking for Samara? They would never stop looking.

Was there hope? Hope is often the only thing one is left with when stripped of everything else.

A few years into Hippo and Natalya's marriage, Hippo's father passed away from a heart ailment, and his mother returned to her village. Initially, she would visit them every fortnight, but over time, her visits became less frequent. For Hippo, life had become a cycle of making ends meet, slaving at his corporate firm and saving a little money to support his mother.

If there were cracks in his relationship with Natalya, Hippo never really sensed them. They seldom met their few friends; most of their college mates had found jobs in other cities and moved out. Apart from a few family gatherings, their social life was non-existent.

Natalya never complained though.

Hippo only began to notice Natalya's eccentricities after their marriage. They seemed to have been inconspicuous before that, probably shrouded under her overly pleasing demeanour. Natalya had taken up part-time work after marriage at her grandfather's publishing house in Pakistan, so frequent visits to the neighbouring country were a given for her. When she wasn't working, she spent hours gardening, talking endlessly to her chrysanthemums and carnations, which Hippo thought was odd.

Though Natalya never complained, that distant look in her eyes grew more pronounced. She was never one to show signs of being jealous. She was never overtly anything. Hippo found it easy to live with her; he hadn't expected much from a wife anyway. As long as she could cook a decent meal and didn't harbour grand expectations, he could live with anyone. He had never envisioned a life full of great luxury and passionate pursuits. He was content being ordinary. He had become a lawyer, an ordinary one at that, and it suited him just fine so long as he could buy groceries for the week, some liquor for the weekend, afford the latest gadgets, save enough money in a month to take care of his mother's groceries as well as have savings for retirement. After his father's passing, there was no one he needed to impress.

His wife didn't have unusual demands. They ordered Chinese and Thai takeout twice a month, and went on a holiday every couple of years—that only when Hippo insisted. And so, after aiming for nothing out of the ordinary, now looking back at THAT night, Hippo thought how extraordinary it had been.

The night Hippo murdered his wife was unlike any other.

In the courtroom, where his fate was about to be sealed by a stern-looking judge about 65 years of age, the memory of that night couldn't be clearer.

Hippo had come home early that evening, at six; Natalya hadn't expected him till nine. She had informed him that she would be at the salon until seven, so he'd expected the house to be empty. But when he came up to the front door, he found it unlocked. *Strange*, he thought. When he heard the sound of Punjabi folk music blaring from the TV in the drawing room, he thought perhaps Natalya had cancelled her salon appointment.

He started climbing the stairs to their bedroom, his mind saturated with a contract he had just reviewed—excise and sales taxes; he felt he could do with a warm shower. But halfway up, he heard muffled voices coming from the room. Curious, he approached cautiously, noticing the door was half open.

He could hear someone crying, and then a voice, which he knew so well—the voice of his wife—in a tone he had never heard before. 'I will get rid of him tonight!' she declared menacingly. 'I have spent a long, arduous, torturous decade and can't take it any more! Just like I took care of that silly girl—what was her name? Ah, Samara! Yes, dear Samara— just like I made her a prisoner of her own dreams, I will kill him. This fool, good-for-nothing, ordinary man will also die in the most ordinary manner! I have already spiked his food with the most basic arson I could lay my hands on! Tsk, Tsk, what a pity. He can't even claim to have had an interesting end.'

She suddenly burst into peals of high-pitched laughter, her long brown hair spilling over her shoulders as her green eyes looked more scornful than ever before. She looked like a witch, brewing her most potent potion.

Hippo stood there for several minutes, stunned. His face had become red, all the blood from every inch of his body rushing to it. At first he thought this was a grotesque dream and tried to shake himself out of it. Maybe this was one of the many nightmares that haunted him following Samara's disappearance, even after all these years. He had even sought therapy; her disappearance had rendered him a mechanical robot, going through the motions of life without actually living it.

He flapped his arms and legs like a baby who had just discovered motion, and then slapped himself on the face. He ran down the stairs, and then out of the house, towards the garage. Inside, right in the centre, lay a heavy iron trunk that Natalya had forbidden him to open. She had told him it held 'memories' of her grandparents, and sharing them made her sad and uncomfortable since they were no more. He grabbed a hammer and struck the rusty lock till it broke apart. He lifted the lid to find the trunk overflowing with letters addressed to him—except they were addressed not to his real name but to 'Hippo Singh'—from Samara. They were dated back five, six, even seven years.

He tore open the envelopes like a man possessed and read five...six...seven...eight of them, tears streaming down his face. There were hundreds of them.

He read the letter from the first year of her captivity, letting out a wail, then a deafening scream—'AAARRGGHHHHHHHHHHHHHHHH!'

The letters overflowed with emotions and questions, questions to him, questions to whoever was reading. In one letter from two years into her disappearance, she had written: *'How are you all now? Are you still looking for me? Did this happen because of my rebellious nature? Did my parents get any of my letters? Maybe they hadn't, seeing that they never replied.'*

The murder itself was quite a simple affair, much smoother than Hippo had thought it could be.

After reading as many of those letters as he could, he had left the house, feeling shattered. Those two and a half hours had felt like an eternity. He roamed the streets trying to put the pieces together in his head, and finally came back to the house at nine, the time she would be expecting him.

Natalya was in the kitchen, humming her favourite song, 'Kal Ho Naa Ho'. They had seen the movie together a few years ago, on one of their rare outings. Natalya had begged him to come home early just so they could make it to the evening show.

'Oh, Natalya, how apt,' Hippo snorted, not realizing he had spoken out loud.

'Oh! Hi honey. You startled me!' Natalya said, her hands

shaking as she stirred something in the pot.

How she hides everything! Hippo thought. *How she has suppressed everything behind those evil green eyes and that perfected fake smile.*

'Startled? By now I'd think nothing would startle you.' His voice dripped sarcasm, a mix of bitterness and forced cheer. 'Did you think I finally ran away and wouldn't come home tonight?'

'Oh, shush,' Natalya squealed in her typical manner. 'Now go freshen up. Dinner will be on the table in two minutes. I made your favourite—mutton biryani!'

The end came down to one bullet, one pull of the trigger of the 9mm rifle he had purchased the same evening. The shot was fired at point-blank range, the muzzle pressed against her lips. It was the part of her face, the one that broke into that distracting smile, that Hippo decided he needed to blast.

But before the murder, there were questions. A lot of them. And she answered most. Perhaps that is why even though that night changed everything for the worse, it also brought the closure Hippo had been searching for for a long and haunting decade. That was the irony of that night. Even in death Natalya hadn't forgotten to turn it into a bitter-sweet irony.

Natalya, his Natalya Begum as she insisted Hippo call her, was the same Meera Samara had befriended in Israel—the same Meera who toured the entire city of Tel Aviv with Samara and the same one who learnt all about her life, her secrets, her dreams and experiences; the same one who heard the real reason why Samara had visited

Israel, something Samara had shared with no one but her new friend Meera, whom she had started trusting with her life.

The story was about Samara's grandmother's Israeli roots. Samara's grandmother had been married to an Israeli, who worked for the government, before Samara's grandfather, a secret her grandmother had told only young Samara. Even her father had no idea. Samara had held this secret close to her heart, telling no one, until she felt a closeness to Meera unlike anything she had ever experienced before. It was as though they were sisters separated at birth.

She heard stories that greatly fascinated her, her grandma's romance in a foreign land on an exchange trip and then marrying the man on a whim. It seemed to Samara that her romanticized version of the world had been passed on genetically!

Natalya had grown up in poverty and hardship in Pakistan, born to parents who had died in a Palestinian refugee camp, just after she was born. The only object that she had was a locket that had been found near her parents' dead bodies. It belonged to the Israeli soldier who had conducted the massive strikes, and inside it was a picture of Samara's grandmother.

Over time, Natalya became obsessed with this picture, lamenting her fate and feeling heartbroken at having missed out on knowing a parent's love. She kept thinking about the woman in the locket and wondering who her loved ones could be. That was when she found Samara, having chanced upon her social media account while searching for her grandmother. The power of technology. She hacked into

Samara's digital life and flooded her feed with pictures of Israel. Little did she know that her hacking skills and stalking skills would finally bring her the vengeance she had imagined in all her twisted fantasies.

Initially, she had only planned to kidnap Samara. The ransom money would be enough to start a life anywhere else; away from the hardships and tumultuous life of Pakistan. Since her foster parents' deaths, she had nothing to go back to there anyway.

It was Samara's stories that changed her mind. Natalya had often yearned for the life she was hearing about. She had never witnessed a life of luxury, security and comfort. Hopping from one orphanage to the next, from one abusive family to the next, her heart was full of hatred and disgust at others' good fortunes.

'Yes, I erased Samara from everywhere. Every month, I went to the mailbox at the Christian missionary, her old home, to intercept her letters before anyone else could find them. He grandmother lived like a princess in the very land my in which forefathers perished—why? Where was the justice in that? Samara thinks her parents are dead—I wrote to her anonymously two years ago. My foolproof plan! Ain't I a genius!' Natalya ranted, her voice charged with zeal, her eyes gleaming with a mad satisfaction. She wasn't confessing out of fear; she was revelling in her victory, as though she were unveiling a masterpiece.

Hippo noticed how her face softened, as if the confession brought her a twisted sense of relief. *Strange, how secrets, no matter how dark or ugly, cannot sit comfortably in any stomach. They churn and churn till they are finally forced out,* thought Hippo just before he pulled the trigger.

The room was silent as the judge's voice echoed through. 'The court pronounces Harpreet Singh guilty of first-degree murder of his wife, beyond reasonable doubt...'

As Harpreet Singh, or Hippo, as he was once known to the world, was being handcuffed and escorted out to carry out his life term in solitary confinement, the prison warden handed him a letter.

'Here. Your mother found this in the mailbox. It was addressed to you; seems to have come from far away. The jury has been kind enough to let you read it—of course, it has been scanned by the authorities.'

Hippo took the yellowed envelope, and before he'd even opened it, he knew. A tear left his eyes and trickled down to his greying beard. The sender's name, Aaliya Begum, was written in the corner—the same name that marked every envelope in the trunk in his garage.

Ten Senses and Sixth Sense

I worked at the Ten Senses Hotel in Bangkok for over a decade—a long time by any standard. A decade in a marriage means you've likely figured out why your spouse annoys you—and how to manoeuvre through these annoyances. No, I am not married, but I have a lot of friends who are, and I have heard them lament enough about these to figure it out. However, working in the same hotel for that long, in Bangkok, was a whole other ball game. Unlike a marriage, it's a love affair that doesn't seem to lose its spark. A love affair with a hotel is better also than that with another person—this one doesn't get jaded.

I never crossed the line with my guests; but I did come across some secrets—an occupational hazard of being an employee at a hotel for that long. I started as a room service waiter at the Ten Senses, a seven-star property in the bustling area of Siam. When I was younger, I did have flings with foreigners during my off time. At that age, anyone would grab the chance to mingle with people from all over the world. But I never got involved with guests, of course.

'Bhalla will never put a foot wrong and that is why he will go far,' my manager, Martha—an amicable woman of 50 who didn't look a day older than 40—would often tell the new trainees. I held a certain reverence for our guests; after all, it was thanks to these guests who gave business to the hotel that I could leave behind my poor life back in a *pind* (village) in Punjab, India.

I always knew I would escape. While my mother, a widow, would make *makki ki roti* (cornmeal flatbread) and *sarson ka saag* (mustard greens curry) on our small *chulha* (clay stove), and the kids would play in the *khets* (farmland) after school, I would be curled up with a comic book—usually *Chacha Chaudhary* or an occasional *Archie* comic smuggled in by my very 'cool' older cousins from Canada. At other times, I would dream of worlds beyond the fields of Punjab; this would often warrant me smacks from my father's older brother, who called me a *kaam chor* (lazy) because he thought dreaming was a waste of time when I could have been helping in the family's khets.

But if only my uncle had read a little more he would have known that 'Dreaming is an act of pure imagination, attesting in all men a creative power, which, if it were available in waking, would make every man a Dante or Shakespeare.' You can search that quote; it's legit, from someone knowledgeable—I even won a debate in 12th grade with it, the only time I won anything.

I didn't always want to work in a hotel in Thailand. I was studying Ghalib and Shakespeare at Delhi University when I realized that hotel management might actually get me closer to the world I dreamt of. Besides, with Instagram and a barrage of wannabe poets flooding the scene, nobody had time for another serious novelist. A few lines and illustrations were all that people could bob their heads these days, staring at their golden fishbowl screens.

I do consider myself very lucky to have landed this job. The pay got me through from the start, and the senior management was kind. In the initial days, I got by with *ka pun ka* (goodbye) and *sawadee ka* (hello), but over time, the hotel sponsored my Thai classes, so I learnt more phrases. The ambience was great, and on most days I got to meet and greet people of different cultures—Australians, British, Saudis, Europeans, Indians, Americans—all flocking to Thailand for cheap but good food, massages, sun and, well, great hospitality.

But there's one thing that haunts me—the occupational hazard I mentioned earlier—knowing guests' secrets. Sometimes, these secrets would land in my lap when I least expected them. There was this one, in particular, which weighed on me more than any other. Let's just say it changed me a lot.

It was a few years ago, and I felt a secret staring at me, literally, from the room-service tray table. I remember being plagued by it for a full two days. At first, I blamed my anxiety and unease on the occupants of Room 909—an Indian couple who had checked in three days earlier. In my mind, I thought, *Trust my own countrymen to do me in*. But that was only the beginning.

The couple were in their late 20s, and from the moment they set foot in the hotel, their 'loved-up' energy was palpable—an understatement, even. Their public displays of affection were so extreme that the man even snuck up behind the woman as they were checking in. During happy hours, he would say things like 'You're the only one for me, forever and ever', putting even the most devoted male penguins at Siam Paragon's Sea World to shame.

But something didn't sit right with him—the way he spoke to everyone else around, never meeting anyone's eyes, a grimace covering his face immediately after he would smile or the way he snapped his fingers at the concierge staff while asking a question. These mannerisms, taken together, made me feel that this man was nothing he appeared to be. Such a man could never be so genuinely 'loved-up'. The couple had a two-week stay, and I saw them often around the hotel.

One day, about halfway through their stay, the man called for room service at 9 p.m., ordering pancakes with whipped cream and maple syrup. Odd for that hour—such an order was usually placed by someone who had either not eaten much the entire day or had drunk a bit too much, or was feeling nervous or anxious about something. A few years into this line of business, you learn to recognize these signs.

When I walked in with the order, the man was in the shower, speaking on the phone, which he had put on speaker mode. I overheard something I shouldn't have.

'Papa, I will propose tonight, I promise.'

'You better, if you want to save our company. Her father has millions. He will only hand it over to his pristine and proper son-in-law.'

'Uff, I know. Why else do you think I am pretending to be in love with her? I am only doing it for you and our business. I cannot stand the sight of her.'

I should have left the tray and walked out, but I stood frozen. As I have already mentioned, I had been privy to a few secrets before, but this one left me genuinely angry.

At the time, I felt I must not take matters into my own hands, even though I really wanted to. Despite the urge to act immediately, I decided to bide my time and waited for the day of the proposal. This fraud of a man had planned the proposal to the hilt. Our award-winning fountain-side Chinese restaurant was set for the occasion, and our 1920s-style Art Deco bar, famous for its martinis, was full. Every evening, a man of average talent and above-average charm would croon hit songs by ABBA, Tina Turner and Elton John—come rain or typhoon, he was there five nights a week, and the guests loved him.

After his two martinis, the fraud-man, ushered his 'beloved' to a corner table, where my colleague Tom stood beaming, ready to take their order. I knew it was proposal night because I had overheard the man making reservations at the restaurant, requesting the best table for a 'special night'.

Call it divine intervention, but I was at the front desk when he called to book. I have always believed in signs, and that felt like one. At least, I convinced myself it was. I assured Martha that I would personally ensure the evening went off perfectly. After all, the gentleman had booked one of our most expensive suites.

I was seething with rage. I wondered how many millions this fraud thought he would inherit with his showy gestures and a luxurious suit to impress a woman who was clearly out of his league. She definitely made one do a double take.

I remembered her vividly from when they checked in—a loud, hearty laugh echoing through the hotel lobby, drawing attention. I was at the front desk and had immediately wondered, *Who is laughing like that? They sound like a happy person.* Then they approached. She had a twinkle in her brown eyes, her brown hair bouncing at her shoulders and her smile showing off most of her teeth.

'Hi, I am Tara!' she had introduced herself enthusiastically, making eye contact. 'What time is happy hours?' she had asked, laughing again.

This woman was not only very attractive, but also seemed to have an infectious energy that put people at ease. Before I could reply, the man had interrupted. 'We have the presidential suite. Hurry up!'

Where she was polite, friendly and cheerful, he felt like he had come to deliver bad news.

'May I have your name again, sir? I asked, matter-of-factly.

'The name's Oberoi. Remember it,' he snapped, barely looking at me.

I despised him from that second. And my intuition, which had never failed me, told me I needed to dig into this man.

He had turned to Tara, wrapping her in a tight hug. Looking deeply into her eyes, he said, 'Baby, I promise you this will be the holiday of a lifetime!'

If I were on the jury for the Oscars, hands down I would have voted for this man. And so, on the night of the proposal, I was on edge. The secret I had overheard weighed heavily on me. But I had made my choice—I had to do something.

Just as Mr Oberoi and Tara took their seats at the beautifully decorated table, an idea struck me. It was risky, but it might just work.

I rushed to the kitchen, my heart pounding, and found Tom overseeing the preparations for the couple's meal. 'Tom, I need you to trust me on this,' I said breathlessly. 'We need to delay their meal. Say it's a chef's special surprise or something—just buy me some time.'

Tom gave me a raised eyebrow, clearly confused, but nodded. 'All right, but you owe me one.'

With his help, I had a few precious minutes to set my plan in motion. I quickly slipped into the staff restroom and pulled out my phone. I'd downloaded an untraceable voice modulator app a few months ago, just for fun—didn't ever think I'd actually use it. I dialled Tara's number, which I had managed to get from the reservation records. I used the modulator to make my voice sound like a concerned woman. 'Hello? Is this Ms Tara?'

'Yes, who is this?' she responded, sounding slightly confused.

'I don't have much time, but there's something you should know. The man you're with, Mr Oberoi, isn't who he seems. He's planning to propose tonight, but it's all a lie—he's only doing it for your money. I heard him confess it to his father. You could check his call logs and messages if you need proof. Please, be careful.'

There was a long pause on the other end, and I could hear her breathing. 'Who are you? Why are you telling me this?' she finally asked.

'I'm just someone who knows,' I replied, keeping my

voice steady. 'Please, just be careful.' I hung up quickly, my heart racing, and hurried back to my duties. I had done what I could—the rest was up to her.

As I returned to the dining area, I saw Tara staring at Mr Oberoi, her face a mask of calm. But I could tell something had shifted. She was no longer leaning into his words, no longer enchanted by his fake charm. She was watching him closely, as if trying to see through him. Their plates sat empty, waiting for the starters I had asked Tom to delay.

Mr Oberoi dropped to one knee, pulling out a ring that sparkled under the restaurant's soft lighting. But before he could speak, Tara interrupted him.

'Wait,' she said, her voice soft but firm. 'There's something I need to say.'

The entire restaurant fell silent, even the singer, who had never before stopped during a set. All eyes were on the couple. Mr Oberoi looked up, confusion flickering in his eyes. 'What is it, darling?'

Tara stood, her eyes hardening. 'I know what this is really about,' she began, her voice carrying across the room. 'I know you're only with me for my father's money. But let me tell you something—you're not the only one two steps ahead.'

Mr Oberoi froze, his face paling, while the guests exchanged curious glances. I watched from the sidelines, my heart pounding, wondering where this was going. This wasn't the reaction I had anticipated.

Tara continued, her voice unwavering. 'You see, I've been playing along too. But not for the reasons you think.

My father doesn't control the money—I do. I've been testing you, and you failed spectacularly.'

The tension in the room was palpable. Mr Oberoi's shock was written all over his face. 'What do you mean?'

Tara smiled, but there was no warmth in it. 'You're a fool, Karan Oberoi. I've known about your plan from the start. I let you believe you were in control to see how far you would go. And now, I know. Let me make this clear—I would never marry someone as deceitful as you.'

She dropped the diamond ring on to the table, the sound of it hitting the wood ringing out in the silence. Guests gasped, some whispering in awe, others visibly bewildered. For a moment, I felt a sense of victory. Tara had exposed him, and I had played a part in it. But then, the unexpected happened. Mr Oberoi rose slowly, his expression shifting from that unconvincing smile he usually put on to a grimace. But this time, the grimace looked more ominous.

'You think you've won?' he spat, his voice low and dangerous. 'You think you can just humiliate me like this?' He lunged forward, knocking over glasses and plates in his fury. Tara stepped back, and with startling agility, grabbed a water pitcher and flung it at him, drenching him from head to toe.

The restaurant staff, including myself, rushed forward to intervene, but it was too late. Mr Oberoi, dripping and humiliated, looked around in disbelief as the restaurant burst into applause. But just as the chaos seemed to reach its peak, the doors of the restaurant swung open, and a group of men in black suits strode in—Tara's bodyguards. She had thought of everything, right down to this final confrontation. The bodyguards moved in quickly, escorting Mr Oberoi out of the restaurant before he could retaliate any further.

The anti-climax hit as the doors closed behind them. The tension that had built up dissipated like a popped balloon, and there was a collective exhale of relief. Tara, still calm and composed, addressed the room with a smile. 'Thank you for your attention, everyone. Dinner is on me tonight.'

The restaurant erupted in cheers and laughter, the earlier drama already turning into a story that would be told for years to come. Tara looked at me, and for a moment, our eyes met. There was a glimmer of recognition, and she nodded slightly, as if acknowledging the role I had played in this whole affair. I stood transfixed. Did she know it was me who'd called?

As the evening wore on, I found myself back at the front desk, reflecting on everything that had happened. I had expected things to go differently, to be the hero who had saved the day. Instead, Tara had proven to be the true hero of her own story—strong, independent and more than capable of fighting her own battles. Yet, I couldn't sleep all night. I had crossed the line.

The next morning, I found a letter in my locker. It was a handwritten note from Tara. 'Thank you for the warning. I already knew, but it meant a lot that someone cared enough to try. You have a good heart. I've arranged a little something for you—check with Martha. Best, Tara.'

Curious, I went to Martha, who handed me an envelope with my name on it. Inside was a letter of recommendation signed by Tara and an invitation to attend a management training programme she had sponsored. It was an opportunity to step up from my current position—a new beginning, a new journey.

And so, my time as a room service waiter at the Ten Senses Hotel came to an end. But it wasn't the end of my story but the beginning of a new chapter, one where I would step out from the shadows and take control of my own destiny—just like Tara had done. Life's unpredictability had given me this opportunity, and I was ready to embrace it.

I wondered how Tara knew it was me who had tipped her. I also wondered if our paths would ever cross again.

Years passed after that fateful night. Thanks to Tara's generous sponsorship of my training programme, I rose through the ranks. I now worked as the assistant manager of the Ten Senses Hotel, overseeing the very restaurant where that unforgettable drama had unfolded. Life had taken a turn for the better, and I often reflected on how a single encounter could change the course of one's destiny.

One warm summer afternoon, while I was checking on the new restaurant's operations near the lobby, a family walked in. There was something about the woman that caught my attention. She was elegantly dressed in a loose summer dress, her brown hair falling just past her shoulders. She had a calm, confident air about her. Walking beside her was a man with a kind smile, and between them, a little boy, no older than three, who held his mother's hand tightly. It was then that I heard *that* laugh—the unmistakable laugh I had heard many years ago.

As they approached the reception, the woman's eyes met mine, and I saw a flicker of recognition. She paused, studying my face, and then her eyes lit up.

'Is it really you?' Tara asked, a smile spreading across her face. 'I can't believe it! It's been so long.'

I nodded, a little taken aback by her warm greeting. 'Yes, it's me. I've moved up in the ranks since we last met.'

'I'm so glad to see you, Bhalla,' she said sincerely. 'This is my husband, Rajiv, and this little guy here is our son, Aarav.'

Rajiv extended his hand with a friendly smile. 'It's a pleasure to meet you. Tara has mentioned the Ten Senses Hotel so many times. I think this place holds a special place in her heart.'

I shook his hand, smiling back. 'The pleasure is ours. Welcome to the Ten Senses.'

A few evenings later, Tara was lingering by the lobby, listening to the soft jazz music that filled the space. I happened to pass by, and decided to ask her the question I'd wondered about all these years. Our eyes met, and it was as if she could read them.

'I bet you've got questions!' she said, like a soothsayer.

I nodded in the affirmative.

'I knew it was you because that night I'd gone down for a late swim to clear my head. Call it a sixth sense, but something wasn't sitting right with me about that relationship for a few days. I had left my swimming goggles in the room, so when I came up to get them, I found the door half open. And there you were, eavesdropping on that idiotic ex-boyfriend of mine, as he ranted about his plans to his father. What a greedy dog! All my apprehensions were confirmed then and there. But let me tell you, the voice modulator app is really shit. You sounded like a squeakier version of yourself! I hope you deleted it after that!'

And just like that, she smiled her hundred-watt smile, tossing her long brown hair behind her slender shoulders. 'Have a great day, and thank you for always taking care of us at the Ten Senses Hotel,' she said, heading towards the exit.

We exchanged another look, and both burst into peals of laughter. Guests around us looked taken aback, probably wondering what an immaculately dressed, attractive guest could have joked about with a slightly scruffy assistant manager.

I never got a chance to thank her for what she had done for me, because the very next day, I fell ill. By the time I was back at work, Tara and her family had left.

When I look back at my career, so many years later, this is definitely one of the highlights. I never met Tara after that, but I often wondered how she was doing. I also wondered, from time to time, if someone was unfortunate enough to cross paths with Mr Oberoi, and if he ever thought of me!

Six Feet of Separation

Every morning, when Lata went out to hang the clothes to dry, she saw him, seated in his wheelchair, reading the newspaper. This happened at 11 a.m. on the dot, except on Saturdays and Sundays, when the bank was closed and her husband, Anil, was home. On weekends, she would be indoors with Anil, either watching TV or making small talk.

Fifteen years ago, Anil and Lata had moved into a two-bedroom apartment in Dhaula Kuan. In the first 10 years, their children, Ria and Rishi, had been young, taking up all her time. But now, Ria was in 10th grade and Rishi in the 12th, which meant that they were in tuition classes straight after school, cramming for their respective board exams most days until 7 p.m. Anil, the branch manager at a local bank, returned home only by 6 p.m. He was a man of few words and precise habits.

Lata had had little choice in marrying Anil. Her parents had heard of him through a local matchmaker, and as the older of two sisters, Lata was arranged to be married at 26—already considered 'over the hill' by society and ageing parents. She had met Anil only once before the wedding, serving him tea with a polite smile, believing it was what he expected of her.

She did not have any complaints. Anil was a good husband by her standards. He paid the bills on time, cared enough for the kids and never treated Lata poorly. He also never complained about her average cooking skills. 'What more could a middle-class woman ask for?' her mother had once asked her, rhetorically, early in their marriage.

Lata had studied until the 12th grade and was skilled in managing a home. Much like with her parents, she and Anil never discussed any career prospects for her. It was assumed that taking care of the children and a household would be sufficient. Lata wasn't a protester or torch-bearer of her dreams in any case.

She first spotted her neighbour—the man in the wheelchair—exactly 10 years ago, on one hot and humid July afternoon. Her morning chores were done, and she had stepped out on to their tiny balcony to catch some fresh air. There he was, in a wheelchair, looking distraught and hopeful at the same time. He looked around the same age as Anil. In that moment, she felt an urge to know his story.

That day, Lata had been feeling a familiar emptiness creeping over her. It had been a few months since she had felt a sense of any real worth. Sure, she took care of the house, and her family seemed to appreciate it, but some days they moved around her as though she were invisible. Anil only seemed to miss her if he couldn't find his tie, Ria if she wanted more ghee on her roti and Rishi if his socks didn't match. Among her family members, Rishi seemed to be the most attuned to her feelings.

'Have a great day, Maa,' he would say, kissing her lightly on the cheek before leaving for school. He seldom forgot to tell his mother to have a good day. They also enjoyed spending time together, mostly chatting about how his day had gone. But as he grew older, more handsome and popular, his phone seemed to buzz constantly. Just when he'd settle down to spend time with her, somebody would invite him for a get-together. 'Maa, I need to go,' he would say, smiling at his phone.

Lata never stopped him. She would smile to herself and feel proud that her son was so 'wanted'. Ria, on the other hand, was a bibliophile—happiest alone in her room, with her books and music to keep her company, when she was home. She was a girl of few words.

For Lata, the years flew by as she poured herself into caring for her family and home. Her days blended together, each one much like the last. Realization of the passage of time came only in sudden spurts—like Ria's last day of middle school, or the first time Rishi brought a girl home for dinner, or when she caught Ria whispering on the phone, chuckling softly under the covers.

Lata loved her family, and she knew they loved her dearly too; declarations of love in their home weren't shouted from the rooftops. However, that particular late afternoon in July, when she first spotted her neighbour in his wheelchair, she felt a void in her chest. It was almost as if the man across from her was also feeling the same. It was strange. They were separated by about six feet, yet she could sense it.

She sat on her balcony and took him in. He appeared engrossed in the newspaper but lingered on the same page for far too long. She could tell that, even though he was seated, he was a tall man—about 6 feet. He had a fair complexion, high cheekbones and large expressive eyes. His eyelashes were long, framing his eyes like wings.

When he finally glanced up from his paper, he noticed Lata staring and smiled, and a dimple appeared on his left cheek. And that was it. It was the kind of smile that made Lata feel alive and attractive—as if she existed! It made her melt and go straight into some sort of paradise. No words were exchanged, yet it felt as if they knew each other from some past life.

Ashamed of her feelings and scared they were visible on her face, Lata hurriedly ran inside, and into her bedroom. She felt a tingling in her heaving chest that travelled all the way down to the middle of her thighs. It was a feeling she hadn't experienced since she was a teenager and had been crushing on a boy in middle school.

But those were the days of raging hormones; she was a married, mature woman now, and with children. Middle-class married women weren't supposed to feel this way—at least that's what she had always thought while growing up, and noticing the lack of sexual affection among the older couples around her. There was companionship, yes, but she had never seen or experienced that 'weak-in-the-knees' attraction between these couples.

Had he always lived here? she wondered later, while preparing dinner.

Anil and Lata did have sex, occasionally; she was aware of his needs and he seemed satisfied in that department. But maybe, owing to a dwindling sense of attraction towards Anil over the years, she seldom felt that her own sexual desires were satisfied; strangely, that never seemed to matter to him. She wasn't sure if he even knew or ever took that into consideration.

On that hot July afternoon, Lata and the man in the wheelchair began a deep relationship. Was it an affair? A friendship? Or an undefined relationship? Lata had pondered the question over the years, never quite finding an answer that satisfied her.

They met daily on their respective balconies, chatting for several hours. Vineet had moved into the flat only a couple of weeks before he and Lata stumbled upon each other. He had been wheelchair-bound for the past 15 years—a result of a massive road accident. He had worked in a car showroom as a salesman. He got fired from the job soon after his accident as his bosses felt that a man who had lost his ability to walk due to a car accident wasn't exactly an ideal car salesman. The irony was too much.

The accident left him in deep despair. Vineet and his wife, Nidhi, who was a schoolteacher, couldn't afford therapy, so there never really was a diagnosis of his despair. He felt he was a burden on his wife, paralysed from the waist below. They would never be able to have children.

Lata and Vineet, like prisoners from their respective towers and feeling the same sense of longing for something they couldn't put a finger on, became fast friends. Days turned into weeks, weeks into years, and their conversations grew richer. They'd chat whenever Lata took a break from her household chores. Vineet's day, other than sunbathing on the balcony, consisted of preparing the evening meal, cleaning the home, buying groceries, and sometimes, very rarely, visiting a friend. He would bring what he had cooked out to the balcony for Lata to take a whiff and, boy, did it always smell good! Lata longed to leap across the balcony into Vineet's house for a cooking lesson.

With Anil, Lata never had much to talk about other than the occasional small talk about faraway relatives, the weather, or bigger concerns like their children and increasing expenses. But with Vineet, it was just the opposite. They spoke about everything—movies they both loved, their spouses (they were both unsure if they loved their respective partners) and dreams that had gone unrealized, like travelling to exotic places. Lata also confided in him the worries she fostered about Ria's precocious ways and Rishi's gullibility. She also boasted about Ria's sharp memory and Rishi's big heart. They shared everything under the sun with each other, pun intended.

Was their friendship becoming something more? It was Vineet who said it first. 'I think I am falling in love with you.' In all her years of marriage, Lata had longed to hear these words, but she had resigned herself to a life where she never would. However, life was full of surprises.

Vineet was more expressive than Lata. Often, they would just stare into each other's faces without saying a word. She longed to put her head in his lap and watch him read and bathe in the sun. But she knew that was too risky; even if Anil had a fixed routine, her children's schedules were anything but predictable and nor was Nidhi's. Her classes would sometimes get switched, and she could be home any time of the day. The first thing that Nidhi would do when she returned home was look for Vineet.

When out on their balconies, Vineet would be facing

Lata, so she developed a kind of cue for him if she saw his wife coming towards the balcony. She would spring up from her armchair, grab the nearest piece of clothing from the line and start flapping it. Sometimes, she'd even yell something harsh like, 'Why do you keep sitting here? Nothing better to do or what?'—playing the part of a mean-spirited, bored housewife. She hoped to seem like an unpleasant, middle-aged woman rather than someone who felt attracted to the man across from her. In reality, nothing could be further from the truth.

Years went by and they continued to share everything with each other—their deepest secrets, biggest regrets and unspoken fears. Lata confided in him her regret about not pursuing further studies and marrying the first man who came to see her, though she had had little say in either matter. Vineet shared his own regret of driving cars fast because speed gave him a thrill. He also confessed to feeling ashamed of not confronting his wife over her affairs; he feared that if he did, she would leave him, his disability making him feel even more vulnerable and unworthy.

At times, they daydreamed about a parallel universe where only they existed. They even joked about eloping, but the thought would quickly dissipate when a knock on the door would bring Rishi or Ria home after a long day. The idea would fade, leaving Lata with a deep, guilty ache. With her growing friendship with Vineet, sex with Anil also became better. Lata fantasized about Vineet when she was in bed with her husband, and for the first time in years, she experienced the thrill of an orgasm. This even left Arun surprised; *He probably thinks he's become better at it with age,*

Lata would chuckle secretly at the thought.

Anil hadn't changed over the years. He still went about his mundane routine as he always had—with clockwork precision. This was the only way Anil knew how to be and he was oblivious to any other way. He never had time to really give his relationships much thought. The demands of his job at the bank kept him occupied and, over the years, he needed to put in longer hours to prove himself against the younger, more qualified employees of the bank. So Anil never came to know about his wife's friendship with Vineet, and Lata also never brought it up.

Once a month, the family would go out together, the four of them, for a movie or a meal. Anil couldn't afford anything more than that. On the other hand, Vineet and Nidhi never seemed to go out, not even once a month. When Vineet and Lata weren't meeting on their balconies, they had another rendezvous point—at the local *sabziwala,* where they would play the part of cordial neighbours. Vineet would help her put her *aloo* and *gobi* inside her bag, his hand brushing hers, causing her to blush like an infatuated schoolgirl. But Lata was far from infatuated—truth be told, they were both deeply in love—one which had somehow survived the test of time and transcended the need for physical intimacy.

The closest they ever came to consummating their love was one afternoon, a couple of years ago. Vineet had dozed off on his balcony and Lata, who was busy dusting her home, smelled something burning, the foul smell wafting through her windows. She rushed out and realized, much to her horror, it was coming from Vineet's apartment.

'Vineet, wake up! Wake up, Vineet!' she shrieked

frantically, but he appeared to be in a deep sleep. She screamed for the security guard outside but there seemed to be no one around. She realized she needed to act fast, and ran down three storeys of her building, out into the compound and up the three storeys of the opposite building, until she reached his apartment.

To her relief, the door was open. She rushed in, following the smell into his kitchen and found the source—the stove was on. Lata turned it off and went to the balcony and woke a very startled Vineet.

'Am I dreaming? Is it really you?' he said, his eyes looking more tired and older than they had ever.

Lata wheeled Vineet inside and told him what happened. They hugged for the first time. What could have been the biggest tragedy in both their lives turned out to be the sweetest day for them. They embraced, oblivious to the world outside, kissing and caressing each other as though to really confirm the moment was truly happening.

They held each other until a loud knock on the door interrupted them. Thankfully, it was only the security guard. Vineet never told his wife about the incident, fearing that Nidhi would prevent him from cooking again. And Lata, of course, told no one.

Vineet passed away peacefully exactly 10 years and 10 days after Lata first saw him on that sunny July afternoon. She had kept a count of their days together. The obituary in the papers read, 'A good husband and son has left us'. If it were up to Lata, she would have added a couple of more words.

For days, Lata wept in secret. She didn't attend the

funeral; after all, why would the next-door woman attend the funeral of a man she supposedly barely knew? There would be too much gossip. But Lata surprised herself when she mustered up the courage, a week after Vineet's death, to ask his wife how he had died.

Nidhi had come out to the balcony. 'Peacefully in his sleep,' she said. Lata noticed how sad Nidhi looked. She realized then that no marriage was ever just black or white. No matter the shortcomings in Nidhi and Vineet's relationship, it appeared that Nidhi had cared deeply for her husband.

The months after Vineet's death were very hard for Lata. Her children didn't live at home any more—Ria had married a few years ago, but lived close by, and Rishi had moved to Mumbai to work as an investment banker.

Lata began spending time at a home for disabled children, and though time kept moving forward, it only truly felt real to her during the milestones—Ria's first child, Anil's retirement, Rishi's marriage.

Surprisingly, in their old age, Anil and Lata discovered a newfound rapport, a friendship, that had never existed during their prime years. *Perhaps it was the occupational hazard of a middle-class life,* thought Lata.

She never stopped thinking about Vineet. She would go out to the balcony every other day, imagining him sitting there. Would she ever tell anyone? Perhaps she would share the story with her grandchildren. But for the time being, she was happy to keep her secret close. Perhaps they would meet again in another place and in another time, and there the distance between them wouldn't be so hard to cover.

Tony de Souza's Date with Death

2018, Monsoon, New Delhi, India

The day Tony had chosen for his suicide wasn't suiting him any more. It clashed with his son, Titoo's, grand musical debut. The 12-year-old had been chosen to play Draupadi in the school's annual function. Tony knew this was Titoo's fantasy—to don a sari and act as the opposite sex. On many occasions, he had seen his son standing in front of his wife Sheila's dresser, wearing her bindi, lipstick and high heels. Titoo, of course, thought no one saw him.

Sheila was always too busy to take notice, attending lunch soirées most days, and Tony, once a hedge fund manager, had made so much money that he took early retirement and now devoted all his time to managing his investments from home. His routine involved tennis at 10 a.m., bridge at noon with the men at the club, followed by lunch with a nice view of the greens. By 3 p.m., he'd be home for his afternoon siesta. The rest of the day was devoted to checking his personal investments.

The de Souzas lived in the coveted Golf Links area of

Delhi. Tony de Souza had married Sheila Kapoor straight out of college, after a whirlwind three years at the prestigious Hindu College. Sheila came from an affluent Punjabi family, and Tony's family was equally respectable—his father a doctor and his mother a high-school teacher. Tony had been their only child—a good kid, a great student, and always careful not to offend his parents or demand too much; after he met Sheila, he looked forward to being a great husband and father.

When he went to ask Mr Kapoor for his daughter's hand in marriage, he had half expected Mr Kapoor to choke on his French wine, perhaps even have a mini heart attack. Tony had heard all about how it was Mr Kapoor's dream and sole ambition to see his only child married to a Punjabi family that was larger than his, both in status and size—literally and figuratively.

Why was it that the quirks you once found endearing in a person, when you were in the height of romantic bliss, fast became irritants after marriage? Tony mulled over this thought one mundane afternoon while working from home. No, this was definitely not what drove him to contemplate suicide. Sheila wasn't that important any more. After 18 years of marriage, they had learnt to live together, without really being together. They had learned to adjust and coexist. After all, they didn't belong to the 'divorce generation'. That was for the Instagram-happy 20-somethings living off the highs of 'likes'. Tony and Sheila were in their 40s; Tony could swear that his iPhone settings were sometimes as mind-boggling to him as they would be to an octogenarian. But would he ever be caught dead admitting that? Maybe only to Titoo, but Titoo didn't have time for his father's technical woes. He was an innocent 12-year-old busy figuring out his identity.

Why was he contemplating suicide? He hadn't even had time to think it through. Last Friday, he had googled 'suicidal thoughts'. What popped up was: 'Suicidal thoughts or suicidal ideation means thinking about or planning suicide. These thoughts can range from a detailed plan to a fleeting consideration. Most people who experience suicidal ideation do not carry through with it, though some may attempt it.'

Tony had slammed his laptop shut. It was almost time for Titoo to be home. After school, Titoo had music practice, he would not return till around 5 p.m.. This gave Tony more time to be alone with his thoughts. Sheila almost always had lunch plans with her friends, and then they would play rummy at someone's house. When it happened at their house, Tony stayed at his penthouse office, which was close by. He couldn't stand meeting her friends—a gregarious but hollow bunch of women whose conversation centred around the latest luxury bags in the market and the latest dilemmas they faced at home with their kids and housemaids.

When had it all changed between them? Tony could not remember. Time had a strange way of altering emotions. It wasn't even that they'd had some huge disagreement. They had just silently agreed to live with their differences. Tony couldn't stand arguments in any case, so it worked well.

At 45, Tony's life had largely gone as he had planned. He had convinced his now father-in-law to allow him to marry his daughter, promising a certain turnover within a decade. Mr Kapoor had particularly been taken by Tony's assertion that with his daughter by his side, any man would become successful and someone to reckon with. Tony did have a way with words.

And now, here he was, contemplating death more than ever before. He also reflected on the highlights of his life—the day he was declared the best hedge fund manager in India by *Forbes*; the honeymoon in Hawaii, where they had gone diving together; the birth of their son Titoo. Titoo had been a plump kid with large eyes and rosy cheeks till he was six. And then, suddenly, he lost all that baby weight. How kids grew up so fast!

Tony was also aware that his desire to take his own life was a selfish one. He always wanted to be in control of things. He feared sickness, old age and not being in control. He was 45, with no medical condition, and aside from the occasional flu, he considered himself quite healthy. But lately, he had become obsessed with life and death. He had watched a video of the Dalai Lama online, where he had said that if one accepts death as a part of life, they will not be afraid. And when it comes for them, if they have lived a meaningful life, they will have no regrets and they will not be afraid.

Death wasn't coming for Tony—he was going to death. It did cross his mind that such a thought was a sin, but then, again, old age and wrinkling and illness terrified him. And he was happy with the life he had already lived.

The time Sheila and Tony spent together was over a brandy at the dining table, after dinner, when Titoo had been tucked into bed. They sat on opposite ends of the long oak table, the distance separating them more than intended. Tony was secretly thankful for the length of that table. Any closer to Sheila, and he was sure she would hear the occasional cuss words he uttered under his breath. On one of these after-dinner over-brandy conversations, Tony had almost spilled out his observations about their son—that Titoo might be more effeminate than other boys, and how he had seen him wearing Sheila's dresses. But every time he thought about broaching the subject, Sheila yawned. That bored yawn that distracted him. And besides, he knew what Sheila would say, anyway. 'It's all my fault,' she would drawl. 'I wanted a girl and kept treating Titoo like one.'

The biggest trouble in our son's life is the dastardly pet name you've given him, Sheila, effeminate or alpha was quite irrelevant, Tony mused, but he knew that it was better to keep these thoughts to himself—anything to avoid his wife's histrionics.

Titoo had been given a perfectly nice name—Tejeshwar—by Sheila's father. Sheila had baby-talked to their son until he was 10, alternating between 'Teju' and 'Titoo'. For reasons unknown, 'Titoo' had stuck.

Tony just wanted his son to be happy. It didn't matter whether Titoo was effeminate or more masculine than Johnny Bravo. Tony decided to postpone the suicide until after the musical. Titoo studied in an all-boys school, and it was common for the school to cast boys in girls' roles. The school could collaborate with the girls' school next door, but they didn't want to. Tony had attended a similar catholic school himself, but for him it had had the opposite effect. He developed a reputation as a ladies' man and a Casanova. He had dated plenty of girls from the neighbouring school until he went to college and met Sheila. It was a pity that he would miss out on Titoo's wonder years.

He had already planned how he was going to do it: it would be a jump. Out of the penthouse. Nobody would be present, so no one would be blamed. That was really important to him. And he would pen a letter. For Titoo. The musical was next Friday, so the jump was planned for the Friday after. Tony had already begun to think about his last few words.

He remembered what the Dalai Lama had said in that video—'If you live a life of integrity—without hurting anyone and helping others—you will have no regrets in the end.' And Tony de Souza, by his own estimation, had been a fairly decent human being. He treated his staff at home well, ensuring that their families were taken care of. Even in his corporate days his employees had seemed more than happy with him. Salaries were always paid on the 6th day of the month, whether the firm had had a good month or not.

Tony thought of his epitaph: 'Here rests a fairly decent human being, son, husband, father and employer. *Forbes* gave him an award one time.'

Who would miss him? Titoo would, he thought. Maybe his bridge friends, when they wouldn't find enough people for a game; and occasionally Sunny Singh, when he wouldn't find a good enough tennis partner.

Such is life, thought Tony. *You are as relevant as your purposeful presence in the lives of others, in any given moment.*

As a child, Tony had always been obsessed with making his mark. In school, he had been keen to impress his teachers, make good friends. And he had succeeded. But years later, how many people from his schooldays did he keep in touch with? Two, on occasion. *No matter how much you strive to be the best version of yourself, do people care only when you are in their immediate vicinity, out of habit?* It made him wonder.

Maybe he was depressed. Tony remembered a line from a TV interview with a leading Bollywood actress: 'I was depressed at the height of my career,' she had said. 'I sought help.'

Tony didn't want to seek help; he just wanted the next thing. Afterlife. He hoped Titoo would forgive him. But he was sane enough to realize one thing—if he did go ahead with it, he required a lot more help than anyone ever could have imagined. That night, he dreamt of the beautiful Bollywood actress. She and Tony were running around trees—she in a red chiffon sari, and he in a matching red linen suit. Palm trees surrounded them, with the serene blue waters sparkling under an equally serene blue sky. He woke up in the morning smiling. Life was beautiful. There was so much to look forward to.

But he still couldn't shake off that feeling—the one that kept pushing him to keep his date with death. He wished nobody would ever experience such a plight. One more thing he couldn't help but wonder was if Sheila would remarry. The amount they talked or the lack of it and the amount they were intimate or the lack of it, she could surely find someone who rated higher in all such 'essentials for a good marriage' departments.

'It cannot be, Tony—good-looking Tony, the man who had it all Tony—depressed? He actually jumped? Took his own life?' Oh, how they would all talk about him for days. What if he was reborn as a fly on the wall, just to witness all they had to say? Wouldn't that be something! Maybe a few newspapers would cover it too. After all, he had been the best hedge fund manager in the country five years ago.

But Tony truly hoped all the publicity and talk would be minimal, for the sake of Sheila and Titoo. His parents were no more. He could only imagine his rotund father-in-law, Mr Kapoor, sipping his fine Japanese whisky with that scruffy expression—now even more scruffy, but tinged with sadness. He wished it could all be avoided. That was, surprisingly, the only part that made him uneasy.

2038, Monsoon, India

He was sitting on the windowsill of his father's penthouse, when his lover, Santiago, whom he had met at an outdoor movie shoot in Grenada, wrapped his arm around him from behind.

'I will never quite understand why he did it,' said Tejeshwar, his voice cracking. 'He was the best father. But in the end, he was selfish for not taking help and leaving me.'

If Tony could hear this, he would have laughed—'Judged for living, judged for dying,' he would have joked. He would have also agreed with his son.

Santiago embraced Tejeshwar tighter. He knew words would never be enough to comfort his love. He was never able to find the right words at such sensitive times.

'I have only good things to remember,' Tejeshwar continued. 'I am the man I am today only because of him. He encouraged me to never be ashamed of my identity.'

'He would have been so proud of you today,' whispered Santiago, caressing Tejeshwar's hair.

'I know, right? I wish he could have heard me dedicate my Best Actor Filmfare award to him.' Tejeshwar sighed, looking at the rain. 'I wish he could have seen us get engaged. To think in his time it was actually a crime in this country!'

The two men looked at each other with relief. Tejeshwar remembered how his father had been so proud of his first role in a play. He could still picture Tony helping him practise walking in a sari. His mother, though trying to appear impressed, had looked so uncomfortable with it all. But it was fine; his father had more than made up for her uneasiness.

Dearest Titoo/Tejeshwar,

I want to tell you today about how proud I am of you. You are growing up to be a gentle, thoughtful young man. On the eve of your musical, I want to wish you luck. I know you will do a great job.

I want you to remember a couple of things in life:

1) You will fall, or people might push you down. Stand up, brush it off and keep going.

2) Never be ashamed of who you are. You are unique. We all are.

3) Never hurt anybody. Even if someone hurts you, do not seek revenge. It will only make you bitter. And bitterness makes us sick. Sickness isn't fun.

4) Respect your relationships. It takes a second to break one and a lifetime to make one.

5) Follow your dreams. You will find many people

on the way telling you not to, but do not give up on chasing them.

6) In life, you will receive both compliments and criticism. Accept them both, but don't let either get to your head too much.

I will always love you. And I am sorry for leaving you so soon. I truly am. I do not expect you to understand—because quite frankly, I don't understand it myself.

Your loving father,
Tony
2018

Tejeshwar couldn't hold back his tears any more. The rain lashed against the windowsill, its sound drowned by his sobs. This was the first time he was sharing the letter his father had written to him with someone other than his mother. Sheila had passed away the previous year, gone in her sleep from a heart attack. She never remarried. In the years following Tony's death, both mother and son rarely brought it up.

Tejeshwar was handed the letter by his mother a week after Tony's funeral. In the first week, Tejeshwar hadn't cried much, still in shock. His mother, on the other hand, had been howling so much that it startled him. He hadn't seen her express such emotion when his father had been alive. He felt like they were all trapped in a surreal musical.

His best and final memory of his father was straight after the musical. The cast received thunderous applause and a standing ovation, and there, in the audience, was Tony, a strapping man of six feet, beaming with joy, clapping the loudest and even jumping slightly. Tejeshwar could have sworn he saw his father's lips moving, and even all these years later he wondered if that had been a strange chant. Maybe a prayer.

The first time that Tejeshwar faced the camera was when he missed his father the most. He remembered the silent reassurances he had received from just a glance at his father's face. Had he ever expressed this to his father, in those tender young years? Not in words, but he was quite certain the message must have been passed on through his hugs.

'Come on, it's time,' Santiago whispered gently. They left the penthouse and got into Tejeshwar's newly purchased Mercedes. The rain had stopped, but in Delhi, even a light rain meant heavy traffic jams. The vehicles on the street let out angry honks, while cows crossed languidly, unbothered by the commotion of people and cars. Street children took the opportunity of the congestion to sell their wilting bunches of flowers.

Somewhere he's happy. He's at peace, thought Titoo, trying to comfort himself. *And today, he is definitely watching.* The Tony de Souza Institute for Mental Health was being unveiled just a few miles away. Tejeshwar couldn't wait to cut the ribbon and open the doors of the institute on the eve of his father's 20th death anniversary.

After the opening ceremony, Santiago and Tejeshwar visited Tony's grave. Tejeshwar laid white carnations near his father's epitaph, which read: *Here lies Tony de Souza— the best son, father, husband, son-in-law and employer. An all-round best human being. We all needed him around a lot longer. We wish we had told him that earlier.*

Natasha's Nod to Her Normal

Natasha was 25, going on 26, but thanks to her baby fat, she didn't look a day over 15. Now, that might have been flattering if it wasn't for podgy, sweaty uncles at parties, who would pull her rosy, plump cheeks and say, 'You've become so grown up!'

This past year, her internship at Watson & Watson, the prestigious ad agency, had left her no time for physical activity. At least her mental faculties were having a field day crafting ads—finally, her wacky sense of humour was being put to good use. Everything was going fine until that fateful evening when her parents decided to visit her in Delhi. She had just completed a month at Watson & Watson and had finally written a few lines that her boss didn't toss into the wastebasket. She was excited to tell her parents about making small but steady strides in a new career, in this new unruly, unsparing city.

The Khannas—her parents—lived in Amritsar, a city once bustling and holy, now a knackered and 'lost glory' version of its former self. It was still holy though, for it was home to the Golden Temple.

Natasha climbed into her Uber, which had pulled up outside her rented flat in Defence Colony. It was June, and even the evenings were a sweltering 37°C. She wore a loose, knee-length kaftan, strategically chosen to disguise the extra kilos that would no doubt prompt her mother to declare that Natasha was going to suffer a heart attack soon. Anything Natasha did or didn't do, was or wasn't, would inevitably become a topic for Mrs Khanna's disapproval.

'Please try "maintaining" at least,' her mother would chide her about her figure. 'You are five-foot-one... Any more weight, and you will look like a duck! I am saying this for your own good!'

True, Natasha was on the shorter side, and had struggled with her weight throughout her life. It was as unpredictable as a yo-yo on a string. 'It's fine, Mom. People like me for my personality. Now how many people can say that!' she would retort with confidence. And it was true. Natasha had plenty of friends—boys, girls, and others not quite decided—and she carried herself confidently. But, of late, even she wasn't happy with her extra pounds. She secretly wished to be called 'pretty', too. Her first and only college boyfriend would often say, 'Natooo, you are so cute, yaar!' She had dumped him when he started saying that too much. It messed with her attempts to channel her 'inner sexy'. Of course, she told him, 'We want different things in life.'

Natasha was meeting her parents at Zing, a Chinese restaurant at the Shaurya Shereton Hotel. Her childhood visits to Delhi would never be complete without a meal at Zing. What had always fascinated her was the restaurant's practice of placing a little goldfish in a bowl on the table for anyone dining alone. That was to give you company and make you feel less alone. How she wished she could dine alone in her favourite restaurant, with a goldfish which would look at her without judgement and offer no advice at all.

She loved her parents, sure, but she knew that the evening would be loaded with unsolicited advice, harsh conversations and wasted worry. For starters, along with her favourite Kung Pao chicken, she would have to serve the horrible truth: her internship was unpaid—at least for the time being.

She could already imagine her parents' reactions. Mrs Khanna would start with, 'What! All your friends have real jobs and you...you...' She would then get distracted by her sweet corn soup, at which point her father would take over.

'And you are flitting from one job to another as if you are still 18!' Mr Khanna would complete voicing his wife's thoughts, like he always did, but in a slightly more bearable fashion.

Natasha had forced Mr Khanna to send her to England to study Economics. Though she had gotten into a good college in Amritsar, she wanted to go abroad and explore what lay beyond her home town's holy horizons. Her father, a well-known businessman in Amritsar, owned a paint factory that employed a few hundred workers. He had set up the factory by himself without ever borrowing a rupee and always paid his workers on time.

Natasha's plan had been to get a good job in banking after college. Although her grades had been decent, the recession hit just as she graduated, forcing her to return to India. When she got back, her father pulled a few strings and managed to secure her a bank job in New Delhi. But the job was mind-numbing, and the hours gruelling. So, she quit. For some time, she joined her father at the paint factory in Amritsar. She didn't mind the job, but making paint had never been a passion, and nobody took the 'boss's daughter' seriously. Of course, it also didn't help that she still looked like a podgy, gawky teenager rather than an adult.

Life in Amritsar was tedious and dull. Most of her school friends had moved away, and the evening soirées, which she accompanied her parents to at their insistence, really got to her. Natasha was convinced that most Indian social gatherings existed mainly to show off material wealth—even by those who didn't have much of it—and to poke noses into others' businesses and personal lives.

She remembered the last party she'd attended, on Diwali. 'When is our Natasha going to find her "Mr Right"?' an aunty had asked, wearing a golden anarkali that was too tight, cinched with a glittering belt that made her look like a giant Diwali hamper you would gift someone. This aunty was one of her mother's 'kitty party friends'.

'So, Natasha beta, we heard you have quit your papa's business? Why didn't you try getting some work experience in England?' her equally nosy husband asked, before Natasha had even digested the first question.

Natasha wondered if she could ask them how much sex they were having. In her mind, the questions they fired at her were just as personal. But she knew better than to say anything. Instead, she had mastered the 'side nod'—tilting her head to one side, shaking it and smiling. She didn't want to answer, so in her mind, she pictured this as a 'respectable' way of taking it all in. It worked; soon enough, the aunties and uncles would spot other unsuspecting 20-somethings like Natasha, and head towards them to fire away their barrage of questions and advice.

The Uber pulled up at the restaurant, and Natasha jumped out hurriedly, almost forgetting her purse and then stumbling on the first step. She could have sworn she saw the driver chuckle after her. *Maybe I should have been a circus clown. I would be their star act, and they would probably pay me extra,* Natasha thought as she ran up the stairs and disappeared inside the hotel.

She spotted her parents inside the restaurant; they had already claimed their usual corner table. *Uh—oh*, she thought. Now they could discuss everything under the sun without anyone overhearing. She was about to make a U-turn and run to the bathroom to call them and say she had acute food poisoning, when she heard, 'Natasha beta! Natasha beta!' It was another aunty dining there. *Great!* She would have to go and meet that aunty now. She walked towards the table, plastering a fake smile and wishing the earth beneath her would open. The aunty was her father's school friend's wife's sister.

'Why does every damn Punjabi know each other in this country?' she muttered under her breath. She headed towards the table and the aunty got up from her seat, grabbing Natasha by the shoulder and blurting out, 'Beta! I just met your parents! They said you are doing some internship in some company? Now, now, beta, I have just suggested a good boy for you. He lives in Sainik Farm! Get married and have some fun!' Before Natasha could react, either in thought or gesture, the aunty flashed a huge smile and returned to her seat.

Aaargh, why do they have to tell everyone everything? she fumed to herself, already mad at her parents. *Now is not the time, Natasha, regain composure,* she told herself. Her parents spotted her just as the aunty had finished her unsolicited advice. She walked over to them, gave them both a hug and slid into the vacant seat.

'How are you, beta?' Mr Khanna asked, extending his hand towards her.

Mrs Khanna patted her shoulder and commented, 'It's very hot in Delhi. Are you managing alright?'

They both seemed very composed. *Odd,* thought Natasha. There was an awkward silence, which stretched for several seconds, leaving her feeling anxious. Natasha stared at the menu for some time, until she finally decided to break the tension. 'So! Did you know that Jack Ma didn't know what he wanted to become till he was 40?'

'Who is Jack's Ma? She had him at 40?' enquired Mrs Khanna, looking alarmed.

'He is a Chinese billionaire!' her father replied, glancing up from the menu. 'And we should know this because...?'

Just then, the waiter arrived, and Natasha let out a huge sigh of relief. Mrs Khanna placed their orders.

'How is the internship coming along?' asked Mr Khanna. Natasha could never tell what her father was really thinking.

'Great, Papa! I am working on the "Save the Ganga

Campaign". My mentor, Mr Dhanuj Kula, is super talented. He just won a gold award for his "It's your life, make it long" ads on TV.'

'Oh, that ad! The one where the guy forgets his wife's birthday or their anniversary, right?' Mrs Khanna piped up. She watched a lot of TV.

'Yes, yes, that one! And he said I'll go places. This is my first poster campaign.' Natasha took out a white sheet from her bag and placed it on the table. It had a scenic picture of a river, with the words 'Rest in Faeces' written across it in big, bold letters. Her parents exchanged uncertain looks with each other.

'Smart, right? He loved it! He said I am definitely going to turn this copywriting internship into a real job by the end of the year.'

'How much are they paying you, beta?' her father asked, his voice softening.

The waiter came back, placing a cola drink in front of Natasha. She took a big gulp, her eyes darting across the restaurant. She noticed an old man sitting at a table with a goldfish bowl. When she looked back at her parents, they were both staring at her expectantly. *Oh Natasha, you aren't getting out of this one.*

'So...Mom, Dad...' she began, clearing her throat mid-sentence. 'Well, they aren't actually paying me...yet! Because I have got the chance to intern under the best copywriter, like I told you. But since I am doing good work, they have promised me a job and...'

'Natasha, when are you going to get serious about your life? Is making jingles all you want to do with it? Papa and

I have decided, enough is enough!' Mrs Khanna finally sounded like her worried, exasperated self.

Her father said nothing, staring down at his water glass. It seemed like her mother would be doing all the talking that night. 'All your friends either have a real job or a boyfriend. Let's face it, you have neither. Now, either turn this into a real job within six months or your dad and I ...'

'Are you going to cut me off?' Natasha squealed.

'No, beta,' her mother said, her tone softer now. 'But we are going to introduce you to some good boys. There is no harm. You aren't serious about anything, really.'

Somehow, hearing her mother's usual exasperated tone comforted Natasha a little. At least all her worries were out in the open.

Her mother's last comment was not entirely untrue. It was true that Natasha had been confused about her career since college. Her parents had supported every decision she made. But advertising finally seemed to be her true calling. 'Mom, I just need 10 months...'

'Beta, okay, take your 10 months. But just be serious about it. When you are serious, others will take you seriously too. If it doesn't work out, think about joining me back at the paint factory, but this time, try being sincere; the rest will follow. You will feel good about it. Wherever you work, put your heart and soul into it, and you won't regret it. In any case, you know we will always support you, no matter what', said Mr Khanna. Sometimes, her father was the rainbow Natasha needed after her mother's words rained down and washed out her dreams.

More than watching paint dry in the factory while they

tested colours, an even bigger nightmare for Natasha was meeting 'guys' through her parents and aunties. Thankfully, the rest of the evening was spent with small talk and sharing trivial anecdotes. Before leaving, Mr Khanna shoved an envelope filled with wads of cash into Natasha's hands. For the first time, she felt guilty that she, her parents' only child, hadn't really 'done' anything to make them proud. She promised she would turn things around soon.

After dinner, the three of them took a cab back to her rented one-bedroom apartment in Defence Colony, where her parents would spend the night before their afternoon flight back to Amritsar the next day. Later that night, her parents' friends, the Malhotras, were coming over. Mr Malhotra had been in college with Mr Khanna. Butter chicken and dal makhani were ordered from Roti Mahal, the iconic restaurant where butter chicken was invented.

The Malhotras and Khannas chatted into the wee hours about their childhood—those 'good old days' when life was simpler and there were fewer distractions because technology was not as advanced. Natasha felt like a child again, enveloped in the familiarity and warmth that only parents can bring with their idiosyncrasies and candid demeanours. At least her mother didn't comment on her weight or the number of naans she had eaten, Natasha thought as she drifted off to sleep.

The next day, Natasha went to work with a renewed sense of purpose.

Ten months passed. Her mother's ultimatum about making her meet boys never materialized. She knew her parents said things for the heck of it. She knew that they would never force her to do or not to anything. It was a harmless trick to get her to be serious about her life and career. And somehow, it always worked; her parents knew her better than she knew herself.

But what was it that truly motivated Natasha to take that internship seriously? Was it her decision to avoid revisiting the potholed roads in Amritsar if all else failed in this big bad city? Was it her need to finally prove that she was more than her papa's prized, chubby Punjabi daughter? Was it her need to prove that jingles were not just jingles but a bunch of lines that could create pure magic and make or break brands? Maybe it was just deciding she needed to grow up and give it everything without feeling like a victim and making excuses for herself, which she had done in the past because she had been too afraid to actually leave the comfort net her parents provided.

At the end of the year, Watson & Watson held its annual awards ceremony. To her delight, Natasha won the 'Best Intern' award for her work on the Save the Ganga campaign with her mentor's guidance. Her parents came down for the event. Her mother wore a new green Banarasi silk sari, and her father wore a green turban to match the sari. They smiled from ear to ear, as though their daughter had won a Lion's Award. The agency also offered Natasha a permanent position with a respectable starting salary.

The next day, Natasha's parents threw a party in Amritsar to celebrate her new job.

'Best Intern! All that is fine, but when is our darling Natasha getting married?' an aunty in her late 60s asked.

'Also beta, you lose some weight, na?' another aunty chimed in.

Natasha had known both women her whole life. Punjabi people's obsession with losing weight and getting married competed with their obsession with butter chicken and rajma chawal. The irony!

Natasha didn't even have to give her standard 'side nod' this time. Her mother had overheard and stepped in. 'My daughter has got the Best Intern Award from a leading international advertising agency. And also a job offer, with her own hard work. She has shown a lot of promise. We couldn't be prouder as parents. Why should she be in a hurry to get married? To become aunties like us sooner rather than later? When the time comes, Natasha will find someone who truly appreciates her, and we will support her decision if she would then want to settle down. Also, stop fat-shaming my daughter.'

Then, as though she hadn't just set the record straight, Mrs Khanna asked the same woman if she would like a refill of her drink. The lady looked slightly stunned, mouth open, and gave no response. Mrs Khanna moved on. Natasha glanced at her mother across the room, who gave her a naughty wink.

Natasha chuckled. Her mother could pick on her about everything, but would pounce like a lioness on anyone who tried to do the same to Natasha. Their family could tick each other off in private but fiercely defend each other in public; that was an unspoken code of conduct of their little family.

In the drawing room, classic Bollywood hits from the '70s played in the background as the guests talked and laughed. Suddenly, 'Mere Sapno Ki Rani' started playing, and Natasha saw her parents dancing together. Mr Khanna was twirling Mrs Khanna, who was blushing like a schoolgirl. A minute later, the song changed and they left each other's embrace just as quickly, getting back to their host duties and pulling others on to the dance floor. *They truly worked like two instruments in a beautifully orchestrated symphony*, Natasha thought, admiring her parents' partnership. *Arranged marriage or love, now that's what I hope to find.*

As the evening wore on, Natasha stepped out on to the patio. The sky stretched in deep purple, and the moon hung low, as a cool breeze blew. For a while, she stood there, admiring the purple sky. It was like an infinite painting and its crown jewel was a glorious crescent moon, around which stars shone like diamonds, forming constellations that lit up the heavens like chandeliers. Other than her family, this is what she missed most about her home town—the stars at night. In Delhi, the smog lay like a blanket over the sky most of the time, hiding its beauty.

Oh so beautiful! Such a temptress, this purple sky! she thought—that is how her colleagues would have described it. *Natasha, you did it. You stuck with it through and didn't go nuts in the process!* a little voice inside her reminded her. Her new role as a copywriter at Watson & Watson would start next month, and she couldn't wait to put into practice all she had learnt in the last 10 months. She was also super excited to take her parents to Zing the next time they visited Delhi. For the first time, dinner would be on her.

In that moment, under the purple sky, she reflected that if she ever found a good life partner and became a parent, she hoped she could be half as good at it as her own had been.

'Where have you been, beta? Everyone is looking for you! Also, my favourite song is on, and I need a good dance partner.' She took her father's outstretched hand and went back inside to join the party.

Rinse, Reveal, Repeat

Rameshwar, or Ram for short, was hard at work at Dhobi Ghat—his place of work for over 15 years. That day, the workload was relatively light, with about 50 saris and 50 salwar kameezes to wash. From his favourite clients, he had three white shirts belonging to Mr Lamba, two white kurtas of Mrs Lamba and their son Manu's school uniform—matching linen beige shirts and trousers. He also had two floral dresses from Mrs Kapadia and a salwar kameez belonging to Mrs Patel. It was Saturday, the day when he delivered the most clothes to their respective owners. With the sun shining brightly, he knew the items would dry quickly, allowing him to make his way to his clients' homes faster. This was the part of the job he enjoyed immensely.

The Dhobi Ghat, a bustling area where many other laundrymen worked, was situated right opposite imposing skyscrapers that housed private residences and offices. Ram often found himself gazing at those skyscrapers, wondering about the lives unfolding within. Every day, around 9 a.m., after he had washed and bleached a considerable number of garments, Ram would watch as young men and women, both his age and older, swarmed into these buildings. They strode in with a sense of purpose that greatly intrigued him. In the afternoons, some of them would step outside, chattering and laughing among themselves, puffing cigarettes and stamping out half-burned cigarette butts with their leather shoes.

After putting his clothes out to dry around noon, Ram allowed himself a short break, often slipping into a reverie. He would imagine standing among those individuals outside their offices, casually smoking a beedi with the same sense of purpose. As the sun began to set, he would watch as these same people—whom he had vicariously lived another life through earlier in the day—zoomed away in their cars. They seemed so different from him. This was the time Ram would return to the Dhobi Ghat, on his third-hand scooter after making the deliveries, ready to call it a day.

One particular skyscraper, which had sprung up only a few years ago, intrigued Ram. Apparently, that giant building—about 25 storeys high—was home to just one family—the richest family in India.

'Do you know there's a helipad on the top floor?' Bittu had remarked, slapping a bed linen hard against the concrete washing slab. Ram hadn't even known what a 'helipad' was until Bittu mentioned it. The look of awe on Bittu's face suggested he'd only recently learnt the word himself.

'There are only six family members but around six hundred servants,' Bunty had chimed in, eyes wide with wonder, as he carefully starched a kurta.

Ram thought it would be cool if he could some day make these '25-storey house neighbours' his clients and perhaps even secure a private tour of the place. Maybe he could become their permanent laundryman and earn a quarter in that ivory tower.

Ram himself lived in a humble one-room lodging at Dhobi Ghat, as did Bittu and Bunty. This life—working at Dhobi Ghat and living around it—was all Ram, Bittu and Bunty had ever known. Many others like them had followed the same path, with their fathers, grandfathers and great-grandfathers having been dhobis before them. The occupation was in their blood.

Ram's clients resided in a housing colony, and were always nice to him. Mrs Lamba would ask if he wanted chai, and if he refused, her maid would bring him a cup anyway, along with two Glucose biscuits. Mrs Patel often handed him a laddoo for the road, while Mr Tripathi, a widower, once even offered him a peg of whisky. Ram had accepted the invite, and the two sat on Mr Tripathi's veranda for hours, chatting and drinking, losing count of the pegs. A few months later, Mr Tripathi remarried, and that kind of invitation never came Ram's way again.

Ram knew people didn't think much of him. Like his name—common throughout India—his profession, washing people's clothes, was also ordinary. Everything about him was commonplace until he started his work. As soon as he began scrubbing a client's shirt, dress or a pair of trousers, a peculiar thing would happen. Ram could sense stories within the fabric. With every scrub, he would catch a faint whiff or a fleeting vision of the garment's last whereabouts and what had happened when the owner wore it. He didn't need anyone's validation; he knew this was a remarkable gift bestowed upon him by the Lord Almighty. He had never told a soul about his powers.

It all began when Rameshwar was 15, the first time he accompanied his father to work at Dhobi Ghat. He had failed the 10th standard for the second time, and his father, growing less agile with each day, needed help. The first item Ram laundered was a checkered shirt belonging to a 30-year-old IT professional named Sahil, who had come to the city from Bihar with big dreams. As Ram scrubbed the shirt, he sensed that the owner had endured a rough time the day before; he could feel Sahil's struggle with the big city.

It was quite a lot for a 15-year-old to process—a newfound ability and a sad story to go with it. No one in his family had ever had any kind of talent, let alone special powers; the only inheritance passed down was that of the washerman's trade.

Thanks to his powers, Ram had uncovered countless stories of his clients over his 15 years of work. He'd sensed the strain of long, gruelling days at work, arguments at home with spouses, dull routines, and even once uncovered a theft. From early on, Ram had decided that no matter what he discovered, he would not let it cloud his judgement or the quality of his work. He intended to carry these secrets to his grave. But lately, he was having a change of heart.

Rumours had spread through Dhobi Ghat that their workspace was under threat from powerful real estate developers. On his delivery rounds, Ram had started to notice numerous banners and billboards springing up around the city. Towering above him were posters of men and women grinning unnaturally, holding gadgets that puzzled him. He knew that most of his clients could afford these latest gizmos, some even boasting about them. One particular poster had unsettled him: 'Latest Samstar Washing Machine and Dryer All-in-One. Flat 50 per cent Discount.' He imagined his clients rushing to buy this machine. What would become of him if they did?

Ram was 30 years old and hoping to marry soon. In fact, he was keen to ask for Meena's hand—she lived in a nearby slum. The loneliness that crept in at the end of each day weighed heavily on him. When his parents were alive, their small home had always felt cramped but comforting. It used to be him, his *amma* and *bapu*, until Bapu passed away from a heart attack three years ago, followed by Amma a year later.

Their modest home provided stable shelter as they didn't have to worry about paying monthly rent. Ram's great-great-grandfather had purchased a permanent dwelling at Dhobi Ghat, which was passed down through the generations. It was just one long room, divided into two sections by a makeshift curtain strung along a long rope down its length. In one corner stood a tiny stove, which made up the kitchen.

After his parents' death Ram realized that the same home, once cramped, was now empty. He yearned to marry and fill it with the warmth and familiarity of family. He had a plan to impress Meena—later that week, he would offer to wash her clothes. Surely that would win her favour! And with his unique powers, he'd gain a glimpse into her daily life and perhaps even a hint of her feelings!

His psychic abilities and the secrets he gleaned from his clients often posed a moral dilemma—should he ever share what he knew? But his hesitation went flying out of the window when one particular billboard was put up across from Dhobi Ghat. It showed a woman looking mighty pleased, a watch strapped to her wrist. The watch was unlike anything Ram had seen. Above her, an enlarged image of the watch displayed a message on its screen: 'How are you today?'

The watch looked like a smaller version of the mobile phone that Kuku, the wealthiest of the dhobis, possessed. *If a tiny watch can now act like a phone, which in turn can act like a computer, it's only a matter of time before my washing skills become redundant. Sooner or later, there's bound to be something better than I am*, he thought. *What if I end up without a job and no money, and Meena rejects my proposal flat out?*

He decided he had to secure an alternative future, just in case. His plan was simple. He would carefully test his abilities by revealing his psychic gift to one client—Mrs Lamba. He would spill the beans on Mr Lamba's activities, which he had discovered while washing his blue cotton shirt last month. Ram hated being the bearer of bad news; at least, he thought it would be bad news for Mrs Lamba.

That evening, he made his way to Happy Housing Colony, a 25-minute journey from Dhobi Ghat. Mrs Lamba's house had a pink door, with a small deity hanging above the entrance. A mat reading 'Welcome' lay on the ground. Ram rang the doorbell, feeling nervous. Mrs Lamba, an attractive woman in her early 30s, opened the door.

'Oh Rameshwar! Thank goodness you are here in time! I need that pink sari for Aarti's sangeet tonight.'

'Mrs Lamba, along with your laundry, I have also come

to deliver some news,' Ram said quietly. She was taken aback—her dhobi wasn't one to make any kind of extra talk.

'Uhhh, sure! Take a seat, Rameshwar.' She pointed to a small stool in the corner of her foyer. Ram sat down, nervously placing his laundry bundle beside him on the floor. He noticed a bookshelf—on one side was a silver-framed wedding photo of Mr and Mrs Lamba, smiling into each other's eyes, and on the other, a matching frame with a picture of Manu jumping in front of the Taj Mahal. For a few seconds, Ram got lost in the bookshelf's contents—stories by Rabindranath Tagore, poetry by Ghalib, a copy of the *Bhagavad Gita*.

'Ram...Ram! Where are you lost? What is it you want to say? Please, hurry!' Mrs Lamba called out, sitting across from him on the sofa.

'Ummm, madam,' Ram began, 'actually, I have never told anyone this. And you may not believe me, but I have a special gift. When I wash the clothes my clients send, I can sense what they did the last time they wore those garments.'

Ram studied Mrs Lamba's face. Her expression had changed from worry to amusement; she seemed to be stifling a laugh. 'Carry on, Ram! I am listening, go on!'

'Okay, ma'am, but promise you won't mind,' he said.

'I promise,' she replied, her amusement now palpable.

'Madam, I am pretty sure that Mr Lamba was intimate with someone the other evening. But it wasn't with a woman. The scent on his collar was from another man. And as I scrubbed his shirt, the whole story played out for me. It seemed like they were in an office.'

Mrs Lamba's expression did not change—no sign of anger, sadness, or shock as Ram had expected. On the contrary, her face held that same amused look, which was now beginning to unsettle him. 'Why are you not upset, madam?' Ram blurted out, jumping up from his stool in confusion.

At that moment, the maid walked in with a tray holding two cups. Mrs Lamba looked up and instructed politely, 'Kamla, ensure we are not bothered for a few minutes, please.'

Kamla nodded obediently, placed the tray on the table and made a hasty retreat. Ram wondered if Kamla had overheard anything. After all, Mrs Lamba didn't entertain her dhobi every day like this; it was usually just a quick cup of tea for Ram in the kitchen, with Kamla watching him suspiciously.

'Ram, I appreciate your concern. And I can't thank you enough for what you have just told me. For some time now, actually a few years, I have had my doubts about my husband's sexuality. But I didn't have the heart to confront him. After all, what reason could I ever give for such a question? But now, thanks to your findings, I can try to get to the truth. And then, I can finally move out of this false marriage.'

Mrs Lamba approached Ram and pressed a bundle of 500-rupee notes into his hand. 'Let this be our secret,' she said politely before exiting the room.

Ram stood transfixed for several seconds until Kamla walked in again. 'Please leave! I need to clean this area,' said the maid, waving her broom.

Ram knew she would never say that to any other guest, but he didn't mind. He felt ecstatic; he had just discovered an alternative profession that could potentially pay him well. On his way back to Dhobi Ghat, he counted the money Mrs Lamba had given him—₹8,000! The next morning he awoke early and swung by Meena's house. He made up a story about wanting to help her family by washing their clothes, a chore he knew Meena often took on. She looked delighted, nodding shyly. Ram couldn't wait to ask for her hand in marriage! After all, this new profession had opened up for him because of her! It would earn him enough to afford Meena as a wife, and together they could move into a new house and start a family.

With these thoughts swirling in his mind, Ram began washing Meena's purple sari—the one he had seen her wear on Diwali. As he dipped the garment in soapy water and scrubbed it gently, he was automatically transported to another time and place.

It was the evening before. He was in a dark cinema hall, with Meena sitting in front of him in the sari. The film playing was the latest release, 'Bilkul Dil' (All Heart). Next to her sat a man to whom she spoke in whispers every few minutes. The scene shifted, and they were outside the cinema hall, with Meena riding pillion on a scooter behind the same man. She rested her head against his back and let one hand play in the breeze. Ram followed them on his scooter, unable to see the man's face.

Then he heard voices. 'Your family will never agree to our marriage,' Meena said to the stranger.

'Then we shall elope,' he replied, his voice familiar to Ram.

It can't be, Ram thought. *I must have gotten it wrong.* He scrubbed the garment furiously, like a man possessed. 'It can't be, it can't be!' he roared.

'Ram! Rameshwar! Stop! What is wrong with you?' yelled Bittu, shaking him.

Ram's stupor broke and he noticed his friend standing in front of him. He tried to regain composure. 'I...I am fine. I think it's the heat,' Ram said, tossing the now torn sari aside as he stood up to leave.

'You need to take a break, Ram. You work too hard. Or better yet, get a girlfriend,' said Bittu.

Ram stared into Bittu's unusually happy face, wishing he would stop talking.

'I am telling you, my friend, it's the best thing. I just made one myself recently,' boasted Bittu, leaning back against the concrete washing pen and spreading his arms towards the sky.

'Made what?' asked Ram quietly.

'A girlfriend, of course!' replied Bittu enthusiastically. 'I took her to the movies last night. You know what's strange? She wore a sari very similar to the one you were washing right now. Poor sari, so aggressive you were, it is totally ruined now!'

Ram knew the answer to the next question he was going to ask, but he asked anyway. 'Did you go for "Bilkul Dil" by any chance?'

'Yes! How did you know? Terrible film. Waste of money. If you do get a girlfriend soon, don't waste your money on such rubbish.' As he spoke, Bittu flapped his outstretched arms like a happy bird, oblivious to the fact that Ram had walked away, heading towards the street across from Dhobi Ghat, where the skyscrapers stood tall, to get a closer look at the people who had always intrigued him.

In Gratitude

To God—who always holds me in His embrace.

To the Universe—for constantly nudging me in the right direction.

To my friends—you know who you are.

To my naysayers—every ounce of disbelief fuelled my determination to achieve.